Black Eden Publications Presents…

W9-DGW-502

The

Future

of the

DOPE GAME

Dalanna Anitra

BLACK EDEN
PUBLICATIONS

BLACK EDEN PUBLICATIONS™

THE FUTURE OF THE DOPE GAME

Editor: Sasha Ravae, Black Eden Editing
Cover Designer: Niyah Solomon, Black Eden Designs

For more information, please visit:
www.blackedenpublications.com.

ISBN: 978-1793902740
United States:
10 9 8 7 6 5 4 3 2 1

The

Future

of the

DOPE GAME

CHAPTER ONE

As I sat in my office, behind a mahogany-colored wooden desk overlooking Downtown San Francisco, all I could think was, *the world is mine*. Anything I put my hands on turned to gold...or money should I say.

I'd just finished up a meeting with BART which ended in them inking a seven-figure contract with my company. I pitched them my ideas on how to modernize their stations, ticket purchase booths, and turnstiles, in turn, making them more convenient for their riders. They loved everything I presented to them, and my knowledge of technology and the implementation of my company's software had everyone in awe.

After the last slide of my PowerPoint, their CEO Robert Raburn gave me a nod letting me know that I'd closed the deal, and the room was all smiles.

Now, standing against the glass window of my office looking down at the city moving so quickly, I couldn't help but reflect on how well everything went. Five-years ago, I would have never imagined that I'd be in big meetings with some of the top companies in the Bay Area, pitching my ideas. Hell, I still couldn't believe they gave me my own corner office that had my name outside the door with an insanely beautiful view to match.

When I was younger, I used to always hear people say, "You can do anything you put your mind to," but I used to think that was such bullshit though. However, now, I was a firm believer in the saying because my life was a true testimony of it. Like anyone else, I thought I would enter the tech industry and secure my little mediocre low-level position, and, truthfully, I would've been just fine with that, but God had other plans for me.

I was the first ever black woman to be president of an Information Technology division in California. My company ProTech provided IT manufacturing services, and I was in charge of it all. These white men were salty as hell when it was announced that Ms. Felicia Anitra Harris, the *only* black woman in the entire company, would be President.

It'd been a year since I was promoted, and it was still such a surreal feeling for me. I walked in this office with my head held high and joy in my heart every day. I love what I do, and through my work, it definitely showed.

For the past five-years, I kept my head down just doing what was asked of me until someone finally took notice. I spent many late sleepless nights and early mornings working on assignments that other people didn't want. I always thought that I needed to work ten-times harder than anyone else just to prove myself. Whether that was just in my mind or not, I finally did it. At 25, I now had my Master's in Information Technology Management, Data Analytics, Cybersecurity, and Information Assurance. I was never not working or researching new ways to perfect my craft.

With BART being my last meeting of the day, I started preparing to leave the office when my co-worker Rachel knocked on my door. I knew it was her because I could see her nosy-ass peeking through the glass that encased my office.

"Come in, Rach…it's open," I said aloud.

"Hey, girl, hey!" With a big contagious smile on her face, she eased my door open.

Rachel was the only co-worker I had who I could actually call a friend. The rest of my company was filled with snobby white men both young and old. Rachel worked down in Accounting but was up here with me any chance she got, keeping me laughing. She stayed inviting me out for drinks or food, but I always turned her down because, truth was, I just didn't fuck with females like that. New friends came with new drama and new bullshit, so I was cool. Our friendship would have to stay in the workplace.

"Hey, girl, wassup? I was just on my way out the door."

"Bitch, you're always on the move. I was going to see if you wanted to come out to dinner with me after work." Poking her bottom lip out, she made a sad face.

Standing before me, her light beige skin had a few pimples that needed to be taken care of, but her perfectly sculpted eyebrows and naturally long lashes directed you to how pretty she actually was. She had long wavy light brown hair and full pouty lips. Wearing a black pencil skirt and a white blouse, she stood there with her hand on her hip as she listened to what I'm sure she was thinking was my bullshit.

"Awww, I'm sorry, boo. It'll have to be another time. My fiancé made plans for us tonight."

Standing behind my desk, unapologetically, I still prepared to leave. Closing my laptop, I threw on my black blazer, grabbed my Birkin, and made my way towards the door, lightly switching my hips as I walked.

"Oh, shit, are you 'bout to get some dick? 'Cause I swear it seems like yo' ass don't ever get no dick...always walking around uptight as hell. Please, on behalf of everyone in the company, tell yo' fiancé to wake that shit up! You better be limping with a smile when you come in this bitch tomorrow. All these white folks may be scared to tell you, but I'ma keep it real." With a smirk on her face, Rachel shrugged her shoulders nonchalantly.

Although, I would never fuck with her outside the office, Rachel was so cool and kept me on my back from laughing. She was a Dominican woman and had a crazy personality with a hot-ass temper to match. The way she talked was always pure comedy for me, but she was a good listener though and was actually really down-to-earth. She made working around all these men just a little bit easier.

"Rachel, carry yo' ass back to yo' desk before I have to fire yo' loud-ass. I'll see you tomorrow." Pushing her out of my office, I closed the door behind me.

"Fine...but promise me you gon' get some dick."

"No, Rach," I started to say, but she cut me off.

"If you don't promise, I'ma say it loud as hell in front of all these white people."

"Rachel, you better fucking no-"

"Felicia, you better get that *puss*-" Before she could even finish her sentence, my hand was over her mouth, and everyone in the office was now suspiciously looking at us.

"Fine, Rachel...fine! I promise," I said through gritted teeth as I removed my hand from over her mouth.

"*Heyyy,* now! That's what I'm talkin 'bout. I want details tomorrow. Clear them cobwebs out and have a good night, chica," she said as she air kissed my cheek and walked away.

Shaking my head, I chuckled lightly to myself. I swear Rachel was just one of those people you couldn't help but love.

As I sauntered towards the elevator, I looked up and around the office. All the men on the floor were so deep in their work that they never even looked up to acknowledge me. It had been like this ever since I first got employed here though. I started off as tech support and worked my way up but rarely ever did my co-workers actually speak to me unless they had to.

These mothafuckas couldn't stand me because I was a woman, a black woman at that, and I was their boss. I worked twice as hard as they did, and, now, I made triple their salaries.

Flipping my hair over my shoulder, I kept walking as I said aloud, "Have a good night, everyone."

Exiting the elevator out into the parking lot, my heels clicked loudly as I walked across the cement floor, headed for my car. On my way home, I just rode under the night sky in silence. It had been a long day, and I just wanted to take the time to thank God for constantly blessing my life.

As I drove down the freeway, lights from the San Francisco bridge illuminated around me. During my commute, I drove over this bridge and on this freeway every day, but, still, these lights amazed me.

"Frisco, Frisco, home of the brave. I don't know 'bout y'all, but we gettin' paid."

Gripping the steering wheel, I spit my city's anthem aloud with pride.

Once I made it to my six-bedroom, two-story home out in Hayward, I parked my gray 2019 Audi A5 in my driveway before heading inside. It was about 7:30 p.m., and the stars were shining against the sky beautifully. Nights like this made me want to go sit in my backyard with a glass of wine and a good book.

As I made my way inside, I didn't see my fiancé's truck, so I assumed he was probably out running last-minute errands before our date tonight. Walking into my house, I kicked off my heels as I closed and locked the door behind me. I was so exhausted from the day I'd had that when my feet touched my plush white carpet, I was ready to lay right there and go to sleep. I was up at 4:30 a.m. preparing for that meeting with BART, and it was all finally catching up with my ass.

I guess it paid off though, I thought, smiling to myself.

As much as I wanted to and as good as a nap sounded, a night with my baby sounded way better. With him being one of the top heroin distributors in the Bay Area and my newfound higher-up status, it was rare that we took a night to spend together.

Continuing back to my room, I instantly peeled off my clothes and hopped straight in the shower. The hot steam filled my lungs as I just stood there for a minute letting the water heat up even more. Grabbing my purple loofah, I lathered a few pumps of Dove Deep Moisture body wash before taking my time washing every inch of my body.

Once I finished up, I walked back out into the room with big steam clouds flowing out of the door behind me.

"Yo' ass tryna make a sauna or take a shower?" I laughed to myself as I heard Tristan's voice in my head. His ass was always complaining about how hot I liked my showers.

I was just about to start drying my body off when I heard vibrating coming from the nightstand on his side of the bed. Walking over to it, I pulled open the drawer and saw that Tristan had left his business phone here. It was weird, but he must have known that he was coming right back.

Not paying it no mind, I put the phone on silent and placed it back in the drawer. I wasn't about to answer it. I needed to get ready for our night. Rachel's annoying-ass was right. I most definitely needed some dick in my life.

Listening to music when getting ready was a necessity, so, walking over to my Beats Pill, I turned it on, and it automatically connected to my phone. My station was always set to one person.

As I lotioned my body, Sevyn Streeter's "Sex on the Ceiling" blared through the room, giving me chills. The fire that was burning between my legs was yearning to be put out.

Tristan's ass better have me climbing up these walls tonight, I thought to myself as I chuckled. This dick appointment was long overdue.

*****

Taking a final look at myself in the huge gold-encrusted full-length mirror that I had in my bedroom, I knew that tonight was going to be a good night. I stood there in an all-black, body hugging, off-the-shoulder gown that had a slit coming down my right leg, revealing just the right amount of thigh. It also had a deep v-cut in the front, exposing my busty D-cup breasts that were probably gonna get me trouble. After taking in my appearance, I decided that the sparkly five-carat diamond necklace that Tristan had gotten me just last month was the perfect accessory to complement my outfit. It was embellished with small diamonds all around, and a center floating diamond made the piece even more magnificent. That paired with the matching earrings were all the accessories I needed.

I wasn't really a fan of makeup, so, tonight, my blemish-free, smooth, chocolate skin would be bare. My lashes had just been filled yesterday, so I added a quick cat eye to my brown almond-shaped eyes, applied some *Poppin'* gloss by Kylie Cosmetics to my full perfectly lined lips, and I was good. Turning around in the mirror, I looked back and saw that my ass was sitting up nice too. I couldn't wait to see the look on Tristan's face when he walked in the house. I knew my baby wouldn't be able to keep his hands off me.

Putting the final touch touches on my outfit, I took a seat on my bed to put on my black open-toed strappy heels. As I stood up, I gave myself, another once over and was sure that I was looking damn good. My wide frame was thick in all the right places, and my little tummy looked almost non-existent in this dress.

Now, finally ready to go, I picked up my phone and saw that it was already 9 o'clock, and Tristan still wasn't home. He hadn't even called to check in with me or to let me know that he'd be running late, so, picking up my phone, I decided to check in with his ass.

Sitting on my bed with my phone in hand, for the fifth time I tried to reach him only to be sent to voicemail each time. Tristan had a habit of getting caught up with work-shit, but he would always let me know that he wouldn't be able to make it. Him just not answering my calls had me thinking he was laid up with a bitch or something.

My thoughts were all over the place, but where else could he be? He had no problem telling me shit about his business, so this didn't feel like it had anything to do with work.

Bringing the phone up to my ear, I was now irritated as hell as I blew him up for the sixth time.

Feeling defeated, I kicked off my heels as I sent him a text.

Me: The one night we get to spend together, you fuck up. I hope whatever the fuck has you tied up was worth it.

I was so excited about tonight and got all dressed up only to be left hanging. I couldn't believe Tristan's ass. As soon as he came through the door, I was finna let him have it.

I was hungry as hell though and apparently wasn't getting that lobster tail I was craving, so, walking into my kitchen, I grabbed my bag of Flamin' Hot Cheetos off my refrigerator and my bottle of peach Cîroc out of my freezer before making my way over to my plush tan-colored loveseat.

Grabbing the remote, I turned the TV on before I searched Google for the number to my favorite pizza place. I wasn't about to starve because this nigga wanted to be stupid.

Drinking straight from the bottle, I tilted my head back and took a big gulp. I might as well make the best of the rest of my night.

CHAPTER TWO

The next morning, I woke up sprawled out on the carpet of my living room with my head pounding. My phone was way across the room as if I had thrown it over there, and the bottle of Cîroc sat empty next to me. Sitting up, I stretched and let out a loud yawn as I stood to my feet. Picking my phone up off the floor and looking at the screen, I rolled my eyes and scrunched my face up in annoyance. Still no missed calls or texts from Tristan. I was actually starting to get worried now.

My fiancé ran the Bay Area's top produce distribution company—Regional Produce. They supplied most of the stores in the Bay Area with fresh and local produce, but that was only a front for all the heroin he and his boys were pushing. Between the two roles, Tristan was always busy, but he made sure to check in with me and keep me updated on everything he had going on. He kept his businesses far apart and always moved smart, so him being in jail didn't even cross my mind. I designed an app for him so that he would be able to manage and keep track of everything that was coming and going in his organizations and from where. Besides, if he was in jail, I'm sure he would've called by now and had me get his lawyer up there.

Tristan wasn't new to this street shit; he knew what he was doing, and rarely did I ever have to worry about him. He was a block boy when I met him, but he worked his way up to being the boss-ass nigga I knew and loved today. He was both book and street smart, and that's what attracted me most to him. He had his Master's in Business and was very intelligent but wouldn't hesitate to bust his gun either. Over the years, he came home many times with the burden of taking a life heavy on his shoulders, but I never judged him 'cause I knew what came with the territory. In this street shit, nobody is ya' friend, and Tristan learned that at an early age. These niggas were constantly gunning for his spot 'cause they saw him shining but not too flossy. His presence alone spoke volumes. Even as a young dude, he was quiet and kept to himself; he was an observer. With his smooth caramel complexion and thick muscular build, if you rubbed him the wrong way, he was either finna beat the breaks off yo' ass or pull his toolie out quicker than you could blink. You didn't hear too many niggas talk about him 'cause he was so lowkey, but the few who knew about him knew he was nothing to play with. Still, these niggas just had to shoot they shot. Every nigga who was bold enough to try to step up though got put down. Tristan didn't tolerate disloyalty or disrespect at all. He had a real short fuse and would bust a nigga's head wide open in an instant.

Making my way to the bathroom, I emptied my full-ass bladder before brushing my teeth and washing my face. After finishing up with my hygiene, I stood in the mirror just admiring my curvaceous frame. Standing at 5'6 with wide hips and an ass that poked out further than most, I was so in love with myself. In my younger years, I was so insecure and always had trouble with embracing my weight. Kids would often call me "fat," and it used to bother me, but, now, I didn't give a fuck. I learned to embrace every single one of my flaws. My nigga told me often that I was perfect to him, so I wasn't worried about it. Besides, my weight was now in all the right places—

my thick-ass thighs and my fat ass. My chubby stomach and slightly flabby arms were still there too, but I loved all of me and so did Tristan

Letting my body air dry, I walked over to the nightstand to check his business phone to try to investigate why the hell he wouldn't've came home last night. Before I could even make it to the drawer though, my own phone started ringing loudly from the dresser, causing me to stop in my tracks. Turning back around, I hurried to grab it, thinking it was Tristan, but it wasn't. It was his friend Bleek. He and Tristan grew up in Oakland together and had been inseparable ever since. He was like a brother to T, but I couldn't understand why the fuck he'd be calling me.

"Hello?" I answered with confusion in my voice.

"Fe, this you?"

"Yeah, it's me, Bleek. Wassup?" I asked, taking a seat on my bed.

"I ain't tryna talk too much over the phone, ma, but I need you to meet me at the basement."

"Bleek, what's…?"

"Felicia, I need you to just come meet me, ma. I'll tell you everything when you get here," he said and then ended the call.

Still sitting asshole naked on my bed, I was left to think only the worst as I got up and threw some clothes on.

Hurrying, I quickly pulled on some panties and fastened my bra before I grabbed some black leggings and a long sleeve t-shirt to match.

After dressing, I slipped into my house shoes, grabbed my keys, and headed straight to the basement.

The basement was an underground bunker that T and Bleek turned into their office. All of their meetings and a bunch of business was conducted there, so I knew exactly where to go. Tristan tried to keep me away from this street shit as much as possible, but, honestly, it was inevitable. The type of relationship that we had allowed no room for secrets or lies. My fiancé was my best friend, and when I wasn't working, just to spend time with him, I would sit in on some of his meetings and calculate numbers while they talked business. I had also developed a software that he and Bleek used to keep track of their dope and what had been distributed to who. When it came time to collect, neither of them did any playing because they knew for sure what they were supposed to be getting in return. If niggas were even a dollar short, they was raising hell.

Finally pulling up to my destination, I grabbed my purse before getting out of my car and walking over the dirt road onto the cool grass. Looking out at all the land that was around me, I was so nervous and stopped to say a silent prayer before I continued on. Pulling open the old barn-style door, I descended the stairs as the door closed behind me.

Once I made it inside, I found all of Tristan's men sitting around a wooden table with solemn expressions planted on their faces. Weed smoke was clouding the room, and there were bottles of Remy and Hennessy on the table with a pack of red cups. The room smelled like expensive cologne and good weed, making me miss my baby even more.

Looking up and noticing that I'd just walked in the room, Bleek was the first to stand up before hanging his head as he walked over to me.

"Wassup, Bleek? Why y'all niggas looking like somebody died...and where the fuck is Tristan? I swear I'm finna kill his ass. The nigga stood me up last night,"

I told him as I smiled playfully, but my smile quickly faded though once I noticed his serious demeanor. "B, what the fuck is going on?" I asked as everyone just sat around silent.

"*Hello?* Y'all mothafuckas ain't got shit to say? I know one of y'all know where he's at."

Making my way over to the table, I looked around at everyone like they were crazy as hell.

"He's gone, Fe," I heard Bleek lowly say from the spot where I was just standing, but I couldn't have heard him right.

"Gone? Where the fuck did he go? I swear if he's laid up with a bitch, and y'all mothafuckas doin' all this just to cover for him, I'm shooting some-mothafuckin'-body," I said to no one in particular as I pulled out my .22 from my purse.

"Now, please, I need somebody to start talkin'…now!" I pleaded while cocking my gun.

"He's gone, Felicia. We were coming from making our rounds, picking up dough like we usually do. I ran into D-Moe's trap out on Seminary to grab the money while T stayed in the car. I was waiting on Moe to come back out with the bag when I heard shots go off right outside the house. I pulled out my piece and ran outside just to make sure it wasn't nobody tryna get at T, but when I made it out there, he was already slumped. I was able to fire a few rounds into the back of the car they were in, but I don't even know who the niggas were. I'm so sorry, Fe."

Standing before me, Bleek looked truly hurt, but something in his tone just didn't sound sincere.

"Come again?" I said like my ears were playing tricks on me.

"He's gone, Felicia."

With open arms, he walked closer, but I stopped him in his tracks.

"Don't fucking touch me, Bleek!"

Moving quickly, I stepped back as tears started to rapidly fall from my eyes. My chest was burning, and I was having a hard time breathing as I inhaled and exhaled deeply trying to calm myself down.

"Where is his...body?" I managed to get out while wiping my face with the back of my hand that held my gun firmly in place.

"I did what I had to do. I wasn't about to go down for some bullshit."

"What the fuck do you mean?" I asked through clenched teeth. I got in his face with fire burning from my eyes as the tears just kept falling.

"I had to leave him. I rode to the back of this warehouse on International, and I left him there. I had no other choice, Felicia," he said, sounding like the bitch I knew he was.

"Tristan would've never done you like that, brah."

Shaking my head, I closed my eyes to try and stop my tears from falling, but that did nothing as more slid down my cheeks.

"Shut shit down, Bleek. Don't nothing move 'til I say so."

Wiping the snot that started to form under my nose, I finally opened my eyes back up to meet his.

"A'ight, I'ma handle it," he said as he nodded his head before turning to leave.

"Now, get the fuck out my husband's shit...all of y'all!" I yelled as one by one they all started to get up and leave out of the basement, making sure to take the alcohol with them.

Once I was alone, I looked around the empty room before I let out a loud scream that I'd been holding back because I didn't want to show any weakness. Falling to my knees, I cried, and I cried hard. I was sobbing so loudly and so uncontrollably that I didn't know if my tears would ever stop falling.

My best friend, the love of my life. This shit just has to be a dream…it can't be true.

Picking up my phone, I dialed his number only to hear his voicemail again.

"You've reached Tristan Combs. Drop a message after the beep," I heard his voice say which caused me to break down even more. I would never get to hear his voice again besides for that message. I would never get to hear him tell me, "I love you, Fe, and no one else." I would never get to see his smile again or rub on his beard. Our late-night smoke sessions would never come around again because he was gone.

Lying on the cold cement floor of the basement, I just cried until I couldn't cry anymore.

CHAPTER THREE

I woke up the next morning with my eyes swollen from crying, and the smell of Tristan's Armani Black cologne seeping from his side of the bed. Trying to hold back my tears, I grabbed his pillow and held it tightly as if it were him. My heart literally felt like it was broken as I looked down at the ring on my finger and just broke down once again.

"Felicia! Fe! Girl, where the hell you at?" I heard my best friend Mikel yell as he made his way to the back of my house. He was the only other person besides me and Tristan who had a key, so I knew it was his ass.

With a big-ass bottle of Hennessy and a bag of snacks in tow, he took one look at me before he dropped the bags and came over to bring me in for a hug as I started crying even harder.

"*Shhhh,* it's gon' be okay. I know you don't wanna hear this shit right now, but he's in a better place, Fe. Tristan wouldn't want yo' ass sitting up here crying like this. He would tell you, 'Stop all that fuckin' crying and let me see that smile,'" he said, mimicking a deep voice, trying to do his best T impersonation.

As the thought of hearing Tristan say those exact words to me came to mind, a smile crept on my face through the tears.

Stepping back from our embrace, Mikel pulled a blunt out of his pocket before lighting it and passing it right to me.

"Here, bitch, calm yo' nerves."

Reluctantly, I took it from him before taking a long pull and inhaling all the smoke, holding it in.

"Yes, bitch, get high," he said as he took a seat next to me and pulled out more weed to roll another blunt.

"I just can't believe he's gone." Closing my eyes, I allowed the tears to just roll down my face.

As the weed to filled my lungs, I held my breath and wished I could just go back in time.

"Hell, I honestly can't believe he's gone either. T just had this untouchable presence about him. I know the niggas who did this shit somewhere feeling real big right about now," he said as he popped open the bottle of Henny and took a sip before passing that over to me too.

I loved my best friend. Without even having to be told, he was here for me.

"How'd you find out anyway?" I asked, tilting my head back, letting the alcohol fall down my throat before scrunching my face up. I really didn't fuck with alcohol, but anything that would even temporarily numb this pain I was feeling, I was trying.

"I ran into Bleek, and he told me what happened and that I should probably come check on you. Plus, they found T's body this morning, and you know how mothafuckas like to talk."

Taking another gulp of the Henny, I zoned out into my thoughts as I felt myself starting to get mad. Kel was right. There was a bitch-ass nigga somewhere sitting up boasting about how he killed my fiancé. It was like I started to feel a burning sensation inside me, and my tears of sadness turned to ones of anger. Tristan had always told me that this was a ruthless game, and niggas would try to constantly take him out, but I never thought any of these mothafuckas would actually succeed.

Getting up to grab my laptop from out of the living room, I came back just as Mikel was sparking up another blunt.

"Wassup, Fe? What you thinking? You looking crazy as fuck with those tears streaming down your face and yo' hair all over yo' head," he laughed to himself as he blew out smoke.

Mikel had been my best friend since we were freshmen in high school, and, now at 25, ain't much changed. Kel being gay brought us a lot of bullshit over the years, but any bitch or nigga who had a problem or wanted smoke could get it. Still to this day, neither of us would hesitate to pop the fuck off.

"I'm 'bout to try and hack into OPD's internal servers and try to get access to the street camera footage from where Tristan was killed. I know I should be able to see somebody's face," I said, making my way over to my desk as I connected my laptop to my desktop so that I could start trying to decode their system.

"Damn, bitch, yo' nerdy-ass is finna get revenge fa yo' man, huh?" he asked as he got up, choking on smoke, holding the blunt out for me to take. This nigga always got extra goofy when he was high.

"I know for a fact that Tristan would want me to find out who they are, so that's exactly what I'm finna do."

Taking the blunt and holding it with my mouth, I continued to type effortlessly.

"What is all this shit, bitch? You on some fucking *Criminal Minds*-ass shit?" Mikel asked, cracking up. Nigga was just as dumb as the fuck.

"Remember that stoner white boy I told you I met in my programming course a few years back?"

"Yeah, why?"

19

"Well, he developed a program that we refer to as the Nix. It allows us to virtually hack into any operating system remotely. On my laptop, I'm doing the coding, and on my desktop, I'm putting in my commands that I'm, in turn…"

"Okay, bitch, that's enough. Just try to find these niggas. I ain't ask for no fuckin' nerdy-ass history lesson," he said, snatching the blunt from my mouth. I'm sure all the codes he was seeing had him thinking I was just typing some bullshit…but if only he knew.

"Yo' dumbass done dropped hella ashes on your laptop and hella shit…just stupid," he said before bending down and blowing them off.

I wasn't paying his ass no mind though. My main focus was finding a path into the police department's operating system.

Taking shot after shot and smoking I don't even know how many blunts, I worked well into the night as I got turnt with my best friend. I'd been doing this shit for so long that weed nor liquor could impair my hacking abilities.

"Fe, that's enough, girl. You can finish in the morning," Mikel tried to tell me, but I wasn't gonna sleep until I found the mothafucka who stole my happily-ever-after away from me.

Ignoring him, I just kept typing away, and before I knew it, the sun was starting to shine through my window, signaling the start of a new day. I couldn't stop now though, I was so close. I could feel it.

As I put the final touches on decoding their password, my hands were cramping and hurting so bad, but I continued anyway until I saw that familiar star looking badge and their signature OPD stamp. Both excitement and relief took over my body as I let out a little scream. I was finally in!

Getting up from behind my desk, I attempted to twerk, but my knees wouldn't allow it. They gave in as soon as I stood to my feet, sending me face first onto the floor because my legs had fallen asleep. I was sitting behind that desk for I don't know how many damn hours, but, finally, I was inside their system.

Stretching and massaging my legs, I laid on the floor laughing to myself as Mikel stirred awake in my bed.

"Bitch, what yo' knock-ass doing on the floor like that?" he asked in a groggy voice, causing me to laugh.

"My legs fell asleep." Whining, I rolled my eyes and continued massaging as Mikel cracked up.

"Bitch, I told ya' dumbass to get up off that computer." Standing over me looking down pitifully, he laughed his ass off as he spoke.

Once I could feel my legs again, I got up off the floor as he was pulling out swishers to roll up a blunt.

"Damn, niggas can't even go brush they teeth without rolling up first, huh?"

Stretching as I stood up, I knew he was cutting his eyes at me.

"Don't play, bitch. You know how I do—OJ and a blunt for breakfast. While I read the paper, finna hit the block, 'bout to see some paper." Rapping Messy Marv's lyrics, he started laughing to himself. "And, tramp, don't act like you ain't finna hit it!" Picking up one of my pillows, he launched it at me as I stood there still not fully feeling my legs.

"Oh, I fa sho wanna hit it. I'm the one with the problems, Craig," I said, mimicking Day-Day from off of *Next Friday*. Mikel looked at me like I was dumb before we both erupted in laughter.

21

"So, I take it you got in? 'Cause I know yo' ass wouldn't be from behind that damn desk if you didn't."

"Yasss, bitch, yasss!" I told him as I did the Nae Nae in celebration. "I swear, best friend, that shit gives me such an adrenaline rush. If I really focused, I know I could hack into anything forreal! 'Cause I'm a boss-ass bitch, bitch, bitch," I joked, doing a lil' twerk.

"Say that shit then!" With the blunt in hand, Mikel passed it before he joined me and started twerking too.

"There is nothing better than getting to do what you love."

A little breathless, I sat down on my bed and inhaled the weed.

"So, do you know the nigga?" he asked just as my phone started ringing on the desk.

Walking over to it, I hurried to answer before the call ended. It was Bleek.

"Hello?" Putting the phone on speaker, I looked over at Mikel before sitting back down on my bed.

"Hey, Fe, how you doin'?" Bleek asked, sounding like he was inhaling smoke himself.

"As good as I can be I guess," I told him as the pain of realizing that I would never get to talk to Tristan again came back to the forefront.

"A'ight, well, I'm glad you in good spirits, but, look…me and T ran this shit together. I know y'all was finna get married and all that bullshit, but this was *our* operation. I know you said to put a stop to everything, but I'm my own man and don't no bitch run me, no disrespect. I'ma handle all this though and make sure you get broke off proper each month, but I got this. Just focus on laying T to rest."

Looking over at Mikel, he was looking like he was finna say something, but I held my hand up, silencing him.

"Yeah, I mean all that sounds good or whatever, but I was actually 'bout to call everyone back to the basement tonight. I found some shit out about the niggas who killed Tristan, and I wanted to run it by you," I told him as I smiled at Kel, hearing Bleek exhale loudly.

"Man…a'ight," he said as if he wanted to say so much more but just ended the call.

Standing up from my bed, I animatedly started mocking him.

"No disrespect but don't no bitch run me," I mimicked in a deep voice as I moved my arms like Bleek would.

"This nigga must not know how I really get down, but he finna find out," I said before taking the weed from Mikel that was now almost down to just a doobie.

After putting the blunt out, I sat back behind my desk and immediately started searching through the files until I found what I needed. Thanking God, I was glad that I could sort everything by date and time because, if not, I would've been here for another day.

Putting my commands in on my desktop, I only needed to go back two days at about 6 p.m. Nervously, I watched the monitor as my heart beat rapidly inside my chest. Pressing *play* on the footage, we watched intently. The street was empty before Bleek and T pulled up smiling and laughing. As Bleek said, Tristan stayed behind while he went inside. Tears rolled down my face as I watched a man boldly run up from behind and empty his clip into the driver's side window as T sat there on his phone helplessly.

Zooming in on his face, I quickly printed out the picture before I felt Mikel come and rub my back. No words needed to be spoken as I cried tears of anger and yearned for revenge.

Still in shock, I sat there staring at the picture with so much hate burning through my heart. Shit was about to get messy, and I only prayed that I didn't let my emotions lead my actions.

CHAPTER FOUR

After getting my head right and taking care of my hygiene, I slipped into a sweat suit that I'd recently bought from a new Bay Area fashion brand called Kill Pain. I loved them because they were more than just a brand; they were a movement, and it was ironic because that's exactly was I was getting ready to go do—kill some of this pain that had been pulling at my heart the last 48-hours.

Both dressed in all-black, Mikel and I rode in my 2019 Range-Rover down the freeway. As we blew blunt after blunt, the car was smoky as hell.

"Bitch, you know you got to blap this!" he yelled out as SOB x RBE's hit "Anti" starting pounding through my speakers.

There were two fifteens in my trunk, causing my car to shake wildly as the beat pounded. Tristan used to always joke and tell me I was like one of his niggas because ever since I was a teenager, my dream car was a Buick Lacrosse on rims with stupid slap in the back. As I got older though, the Buick turned to Benz and other luxury cars, but my love for music never died because in all three of the cars I owned, I had extra beat and amps to heighten the sound.

"Loud when we smokin', lil' dope we don't match that. Any sucka nigga slidin' through gettin' clapped at. House lick, we runnin' through that bitch like it's FasTrak. Remember all them days when I was broke, but I'm past that."

Rapping along to the song, Mikel and I were lit as fuck as we pulled up to the basement. After parking my car, we both just sat there for a second high as hell before we looked at each other and broke out laughing.

"Bitch, I'm high as fuck." With his eyes red and glossy, Mikel looked over at me, and I knew he wasn't lying.

"Me too, but let's just go handle this shit so we can bounce."

Reaching under my seat, I pulled out my custom-made black and pink nine-millimeter. I pulled the bullets out of the middle console and loaded my bitch before cocking it and placing it in my bag.

"You ready?" I asked Mikel as I looked over at him to see him checking his .45 to make sure it was locked and loaded too.

"The real question is are these niggas ready for us? Let's go, bitch."

Tucking his gun in the back of his pants, Mikel fixed his jacket before he closed the door.

Stepping out the car with a heavy heart, I looked around at the land that was passed down to Tristan from his grandfather. The basement was located in Rockridge, a little city on the outside of Oakland. There was an old wooden house with a big "ol porch that we always talked about rebuilding from the ground up.

Shaking away the tears that were threatening to fall, I followed behind Mikel as he opened the door and descended down the stairs.

All of Tristan's closest men were in attendance just like they had been the day before. The room seemed to get eerily quiet as Mikel and I came and stood before everyone.

"So, I'm sure you are all wondering why I called you back here so soon…last night, I was able to get a picture of the man who killed T. How I got it is none of your concern, but what I do wanna know is who knows this nigga?"

Pulling the picture from out of my purse, I unfolded it so that everyone could see. Moving around the table, I let everyone get a good look at the image before returning to the center of the room standing back beside Mikel.

"*None* of y'all niggas know who this mothafucka is?" Pausing for a second, I waited for someone to speak up, but no one did. "Please, everybody, don't speak all at once." With sarcasm oozing from my voice, I shook my head. "Every last one of y'all make moves all over the Bay, and *nobody* knows nothing? Are y'all forreal? Come on now, I know y'all done heard something."

With pleading eyes, I came and stood directly in front of the table, slamming the picture down in the middle of it.

Standing up from his seat, Bleek swaggered over to where I stood with a mug on his face that let me know I was finna have to check his ass.

"Felicia, we respect you and all that good shit, ma; however, we don't need no bitch coming up in here tryna question us like we the enemy. We don't know that nigga, and we don't need help from no bitch trying to find him. So, why don't you just go on home and paint ya' nails or something while the big boys handle this?" he told me as a cocky smirk crept onto his handsome face.

Bleek was truthfully fine as hell. He had a dark caramel complexion and a full thick beard with bright emerald green eyes. His thick muscular frame would intimidate even the hardest of men but not me. He pumped *no* fear in my heart.

Standing straight up and removing my hand from my hip, I walked right in front of him...so close that I knew he could feel me breathing on his skin as we stood face-to-face.

"Firstly, I'm not gon' be too many more bitches, mothafucka," I said as I pulled my nine from my purse and held it at my side. "Don't let my intelligence or the fact that I'm a woman fool you. T been showed me how to buss this thing, and, trust, I won't hesitate to lay a*nybody* down. In case you done forgot already, this is *Tristan's* shit. It's his blood, sweat, and tears that got all y'all mothafuckas where y'all at today. Bleek, you know this shit firsthand, so the fact that you tryna dismiss me like I'm just some side bitch or some shit is real disrespectful. You know how my nigga got down. Anything that was his is mine, so you can either get yo' feelings in line and sit yo' ass back down, or we can get shit poppin'. The choice is yours forreal," I said as I took a step back and checked the safety on my gun for emphasis. Mothafuckas loved to take my kindness for weakness.

"I always told T he was crazy as fuck for wifin' yo' fat-ass." Chuckling to himself, this fool was really amused. Everyone else in the room just sat back quietly, intently watching everything unfold.

Joining Bleek in laughter, I looked back at Mikel who started laughing too 'cause he already knew what I was on. Animatedly laughing, I started holding my stomach being hella extra as I saw Bleek reach for his gun. Everything happened so fast as I quickly brought my gun in front of me, firing off two shots that instantly dropped Bleek to the floor.

POP! POP!

The sound of my nine going off echoed loudly throughout the small room.

Whether he was just pulling that bitch out for effect or planning on using it, we may never know 'cause my reflexes were quick as fuck. Bleek's blood was rapidly seeping from his wounds and pooling around him as awkward silence filled the basement, and all eyes were on me.

I never actually killed anyone before but holding the gun in my hand and looking at Bleek's body there on the floor, I was feeling the last thing I expected to feel— powerful.

Bringing a wide grin to my face, I glanced back at Mikel who wore a shocked look on his, standing with his arms crossed before I turned my attention back to the rest of the men in the room. Looking around, they all wore flashy chains and big diamond earrings almost the size of rocks. They all sported the latest clothes and drove the latest whips. To me, all that was clown shit though. Money meant nothing if there was no loyalty behind it. We were indeed about to keep getting this money 'cause I knew that's what Tristan would've wanted me to do, but I needed to know where these niggas' loyalties lied first.

"Well, now that we got that shit out the way, let's really get down to business," I said as I nonchalantly stood next to Bleek's now lifeless body. "Is there anything else anyone would like to get off their chests?" I asked before I paused and awaited any responses. Silence. "Okay, so, business will be put on hold until we lay Tristan to rest. I know you niggas been eating, so y'all will be good a few more days. Whatever y'all got right now, just hold onto it, and I promise you,

29

everything will be back in motion once Tristan has been properly laid to rest. I ain't mean to come in here like I'm just tryna Deebo y'all, but y'all know for a fact that T wouldn't't've wanted this shit any other way. I'ma hold it down and make sure everybody keeps eating I promise you. I just need y'all to rock for me, and we gon' get this money and keep doing this shit in T's honor," I told them, and a few dudes nodded their heads in approval.

"You know we got yo' back, Fe!" Jacari said as he stood up and came and gave me a quick hug. "We know how much Tristan loved yo' ass. If he was gon' pass this shit down to anybody, it would've been you. As smart as you are, I know you ain't gon' do shit but elevate us. We with you, mama," he said as he nodded his head in respect, "And, I never liked this nigga Bleek any-damn-way." Acting like he was kicking Bleek's body, Jacari had the whole room crackin' up.

Cari ran shit out in Richmond. I had only met him a few times when I would occasionally ride with Tristan, but, just that quick, he'd proven his loyalty to me.

One by one, all the other men got up and came to hug me, telling me to stay strong. Our bond had just been solidified, and once we paid our respects to Tristan, it was back to business as usual.

"Now that I know y'all gon' ride for me like I'ma ride for y'all, I gotta start making these funeral arrangements and shit. If y'all need anything, don't hesitate to hit me up. I got T's phone. Anything y'all need, I'm here," I said as everyone nodded their heads in acknowledgement before filing out the door.

"Damn, bitch, I didn't know you was gon' all the way off this nigga. I just thought you was gon' tap his leg or something to let him know you wasn't playing. Yo' damn brothers done turned yo' ass into a whole man 'cause, bitch, even I would've been scared, and you ain't even flinch," Mikel said once everyone was gone, slowly walking over to Bleek's body, causing me to laugh.

"Shut yo' soft-ass up. I had to let these niggas know that there ain't a weak bone in my body. I can run with the best of 'em and bust my gun like they do. I had to prove myself," I said as I shrugged my shoulders.

Pulling out Tristan's phone, I scrolled through his contacts until I found *The Cleanup Crew* and dialed the number. Answering on the first ring, Carlos said very little as he listened to where he was needed before ending the call.

"Sounds to me like you was talking to yourself," Mikel joked as he stood by playing with his fingernails.

"Nah, I wasn't. Let's get out of here though. I need to go see Mama Combs," I told him as I walked towards the door.

"Mama Combs" was what I called Tristan's mother. I knew that she was losing her mind right now after finding out that someone had taken her baby boy, and I was honestly dreading this encounter. I'd been trying not to think about everything and just keep myself busy, but I knew that once I saw her, there would be no more hiding. Together, we would be a hysterical mess, and I just wasn't looking forward to it.

Nightfall was slowly approaching, and the sun had almost completely set. After dropping Mikel off to his car, I didn't even go inside my house. I headed straight for Alameda where Mama C lived.

As I rode down the freeway thinking about how quickly life had taken Tristan away from me, tears started to silently slide down my cheeks.

"You gotta hope for the best and be prepared for the worst, ma," I could hear him say just like he always would.

Nothing could've prepared me for this though. We were just planning our wedding and talking about having our first child together. How could I accept that he was really gone? I swear I wasn't gon' sleep right 'til I knew that the niggas who did this had been taken care of. My life would never be the same because of them. I would never get to marry my best friend.

Pulling into the driveway of Mama Combs' single-story home, I wiped my tears away before I got out and let the cool Bay Area air whip across my face, causing my ponytail to blow in the wind. Looking at my reflection in my car, I knew that I looked a mess. My hair was up in this messy ponytail, and it desperately needed to be combed. Luckily, Mikel made my shit look as natural as possible, so you couldn't tell nobody this wasn't my shit.

Running my hands over my hoodie trying to rub out some of the wrinkles, I walked up to the front door with my head held low. Reaching up to ring the doorbell, I stood back waiting until I saw Mama C approach the door through the glass. She bore a heartbreaking expression as she pulled the door open and stood before me. Like Tristan, she had golden brown eyes and a smooth caramel complexion. Her hair was what I liked to call salt-and-pepper-colored because it was still her natural jet-black color with a few grays mixed in.

"Felicia?" she asked with hurt evident in her tone that caused tears to fall from my eyes yet again.

"Yes, ma'am, it's me," I said as I walked up to her petite frame and pulled her in for a hug.

Standing in her doorway, no words were spoken as we both held each other and cried for the loss that we would never forget. Tristan was so honest and loving. I always said they were two of his best qualities because I never had to question his love for me. If he felt a certain way, he had no problem speaking his mind, and he went hard in the paint for those he loved. There was nothing too much or too big for his mama. Anything she wanted, she knew all she had to do was call her baby boy, and he was gonna make it happen. We'd spent many Sunday dinners in this house, and T had been raised here. I knew for a fact that, if nowhere else, Tristan's presence would be felt here.

Pulling away from our embrace with a wet face, I kept my arm around Mama Combs as we made our way inside and took a seat on her plush forest green loveseat. With tears still streaming down both our faces, we just consoled each other until we were finally ready to talk.

CHAPTER FIVE

I ended up staying the night with Mama Combs. We stayed up late sipping wine while crying, laughing, and reminiscing about the man Tristan was. When morning finally came, we got up and did the last thing either of us wanted to do. We went down to the coroner's office and identified T's body. The image of him lying lifelessly on that cold piece of steel would be one I would never forget.

After seeing his face, Mama Combs excused herself as she tried to control her loud sobs, leaving me standing there alone in the room. With tears silently running down my face, I made my way over to the table trying to steady my balance. I'd been trying to stay strong for both me and Mama Combs, but I could no longer hold back.

Looking down at the love of my life, I let out a gut-wrenching scream as I hugged his lifeless body.

Kissing his cheek, I whispered, "Their days are numbered, bae. I promise you."

Walking out of the room with my eyes puffy, I felt like I was in a daze as I helped Mama Combs up before we wearily exited the building.

With so much to still get done, our day would not end here. The next place we were headed was Fouché's Hudson Funeral Home out in Oakland. Mama C was adamant about letting them help us plan Tristan's funeral, so that's what we were gonna do.

With my heart heavy and so much on my mind, we rode in silence the whole way there.

"Your destination is on the right," my GPS said aloud as I pulled into the parking lot of the old worn-down white building.

The first thing that came to my mind was *oh, hell no*, but I kept my thoughts to myself as I helped Mama C out the car, and we proceeded inside.

I never had to plan a funeral before, so I was going to let her do all the talking, and I would just take care of the expenses.

Once inside the building, my skepticism was slightly eased as we walked across the thick burgundy carpet and were greeted by a lanky dark-skinned old man who limped his way over to us.

"Welcome to Fouché's. I'm sorry we have to meet under these circumstances," he said, sounding like he had something stuck in his throat. His voice was so raspy and scratchy that I was ready to walk right out the damn door. I didn't need to hear no more.

"Y'all must be the family of that young man I saw on the new last night," he said, causing my suspicions to rise.

Niggas die every day, B, I thought to myself as I looked at this cat skeptically. How the fuck did he know we were Tristan's family?

Not saying another word, I planned to be quiet the whole meeting so that I could really see what this mothafucka was all about. He had already rubbed me the wrong way, and we hadn't even been here twenty-minutes yet.

After introductions were made, we followed behind him to what was his office I assumed. Walking inside the room, he rounded his desk and took a seat in his plush office chair before spinning around to face us. The way his Cappuccino-colored desk shined, you could just tell that it was expensive.

"I'm so sorry for y'all's loss," he continued, "I want to hopefully make this process as easy as possible for you guys."

"Thank you. We appreciate that," Mama Combs told him as she quickly glanced over at me in my seat glaring his ass down before turning her attention back to him.

For the next hour-and-a-half, I sat listening to how Mama C wanted everything, and for the most part, I was cool with everything she ordered. At the end of the day, Tristan was her baby, and I felt like however she wanted to lay her child to rest should've been left up to her. The only problem I had was, for some reason, I didn't trust this funeral director. I wasn't 'bout to mention it to Mama C and bring her anymore stress, but I was definitely gonna keep my eye on that mothafucka.

Pulling up to Tristan's family home, I got out, walking with Mama C up to her front door before we said our goodbyes.

As I rode down the freeway, I was so happy to be alone. Thoughts of Tristan's lifeless body were still flashing through my mind as if they were burned into my memory. As my thoughts raced, I picked up speed so that I could hurry home. I was in desperate need of a shower and a blunt. I had to calm my nerves. There was just so much shit on my mind.

I emailed the CEO of my company yesterday letting him know all that had happened these past few days, and he told me that I could take as much time as I needed. I was happy that he was so understanding because, now, my job was one thing less thing I needed to stress about.

Exiting off the freeway in Hayward, thoughts of Tristan's business and if I could really do this shit on my own clouded my mind. I was never one to doubt myself, but I knew that this shit was a whole 'nother playing field than what I was used to. Many times before, I'd heard Tristan tell me that the dope game was ruthless as fuck but never had I personally experienced it myself. He would always put emphasis on the fact that there were no friends in this shit and that you couldn't trust nobody. I used to always think he was being extra, but he wasn't exaggerating like I thought he was 'cause, true to his word, someone had ruthlessly taken his life away from him in broad daylight.

Us living two completely different lifestyles always left one of us wanting to know what the other was doing. When he would see me coding, I would break it down for him. And, when I would see him cooking up work, he would break it down for me. He showed me the ins and outs of the game solely because I was curious at first, but, then, it turned into more. I knew how to cook, cut, and sell dope, and if needed to, I knew how to discreetly transport at least ten keys. Because of the life he led, T knew that niggas were gunning for him and could possibly find out where he laid his head, so he made sure that I also knew how to use a gun. From something as small as a deuce-deuce to even heavier artillery like an AK, I knew how to take them apart and put them back together as well as load and shoot them. Tristan had shown me all this, just to prepare me for if someone succeeded in taking his life. We would've never imagined that day would come so quickly though.

Bleek was T's boy and all, but he never had any intention on passing his business down to him. This was something that Tristan wanted to keep in the family and one day pass down to his sons if they wanted it...the ones we'd never get to have.

"No outsiders allowed," I could hear him say as clear as day as if he was riding right along with me.

Smiling to myself, I knew that with T guiding my steps and my knowledge in technology, I was finna take this street shit to another level.

After pulling into my driveway, I hopped out my car and just stood there gazing at my house. I could still hear Tristan's voice in my head as we shopped around looking for the perfect house that we could raise a family in.

"Man, you know I don't care about this shit. Whichever one makes you happy is gon' make me happy," he told me after I asked him which one he thought was the best. After careful consideration, I ended up deciding on this six-bedroom, four-bath beauty. It was newly built, and everything inside was brand-new. The plush carpet though is what ultimately sold me 'cause I imagined myself walking barefoot across it. Now, a year later, I couldn't believe that I was walking inside of it alone. I couldn't comprehend the fact that my family would never get a chance to be built here, that I'd never get to come back home with the love of my life to this house. Nothing was the same, and it never would be again.

Finally walking up to my door, I used my key and let myself in before I locked it behind me. I was taking off my shoes when I heard my phone chime with an incoming message from my purse. Pulling it out, I saw that it was from Mikel before I opened it.

Mikel: *Hey, bitch, I just wanted to check on you. I know you're strong as hell, so I'm not really worried, but this is what besties do. If you need me, you know I'm only*

*a call away. I'll probably stop by tomorrow anyway, but
I love you, girl...keep yo' head up!*

After reading his message, I couldn't help but smile.
My best friend was really the shit forreal. I loved the fuck
out his crazy-ass, and there was no one else on this earth
who I trusted more than him.

Walking back to my bedroom, I peeled my clothes
off my thick frame before walking over and turning the
crystal handle to run my bath. After the trip to the
coroner's office and the meeting at the funeral home, I
just needed to relax.

Naked as fuck, I walked to the kitchen to get my
bottle of Stella Rosa wine before returning back to my
bedroom. Steam was rising from my bath water just the
way I liked it. Eager to get in, and with no cup, me and
my bottle of wine slid into the hot water as I reached up
and turned on the jets. All I was missing was a blunt, but
I didn't feel like getting out to go roll one.

Resting my head back against my neck pillow, I let
the steamy hot water and jets soothe my body as I took a
sip of my wine straight from the bottle. Since I'd found
out about Tristan passing, I hadn't been able to sleep that
well. I'd been getting in two-, maybe three-hours at the
most, every day.

Getting comfortable in the water, I closed my eyes as
memories of Tristan flooded my mind.

*****

Confused as hell, I woke up still sitting in a tub of
cold water not knowing how much time had passed.
Draining the tub, I carefully stepped out before I went

and checked my phone. It was 3 a.m.! I slept in that tub for five-hours, and I didn't even wash up.

Shaking my head, I turned on the shower and actually washed my ass this time. Once I finished up, I applied a little cocoa butter oil all over my body and climbed in bed naked as the day I was born. I was just about to lay down when I realized I hadn't charged Tristan's business phone. None of his men would have been able to reach me if they needed to.

Jumping back up, I hurried over to my nightstand. There was no battery left, so plugging the charger into the wall, I waited for the phone to power on. Grabbing my laptop, I decided that I could also catch up on some work. Sitting up in my bed, I pulled the covers over me before placing it in my lap. I knew it would be cold as hell if I placed it on my bare skin.

Once the phone was powered back on, a bunch of notifications started coming through. Scrolling all the way down to the last unread text, I worked my way up reading every single message.

A lot of them were from the men on Tristan's payroll asking about when they'd receive more product or when it be good to get shit back moving. Another one was from his connect Emiliano. His message caused my eyes to bulge out of my head. He and Tristan had a meeting set up for tomorrow. Obviously, he had no clue about T's murder. Staring down at the phone, my heart pounded. I met Emiliano once before and knew that he was nothing to play with. A man of his caliber would kill a mothafucka in a heartbeat and not lose any sleep over it. When I went with Tristan to meet up with him the last time, he had men stationed at the entrance and every corner of the warehouse that they frequently met up at. You would've thought he was a government official the way he was guarded. His presence alone screamed money, and I didn't know if he'd be willing to do business with a small fish like me. A lot of men were skeptical about going into business with women, thinking that we all are too emotional and irrational, but, in my case, that couldn't be further from the truth. I was precise and level-headed, ambitious, and I didn't take shit from anyone...male or female.

I was just going to have to show up to the meeting and pray that Emiliano would help me carry on this business.

Calming my nerves, I picked the phone back up and proceeded to read through the rest of the missed text messages. Everything else was all basically bullshit. Everybody was asking when we'd get shit back moving.

The last few messages were from Jacari. He was checking to see how I was doing and when the funeral would be. He also asked if I needed anything which I thought was sweet, but I would never ask another man for shit outta respect to Tristan. Besides, I made my own bread and would never need a nigga for shit anyhow.

After replying to Cari's texts...although, it was nearly four o'clock in the morning, I thanked him for checking on me and let him know that everything was all good, and that the funeral was set for Monday.

Setting the phone down, I picked up my laptop so that I could go through my work emails. I knew that I probably had about a thousand unread ones to catch up on.

After finishing up with a bit of work, the sun started shining through my window, and I knew I wouldn't be getting anymore sleep than what I'd got while I was in the bath earlier. I was cool with that though 'cause me staying busy kept my mind off Tristan and the tears from falling.

The meeting with Emiliano was today, so I knew that I was gonna have to take at least $500,000 from the in-house safe that T kept in our closet and go handle business. I was nervous, and I didn't want to go alone, but I also didn't want to raise any red flags.

Making my way over to our walk-in closet, I searched the floor until I found two black duffle bags that I knew would be able to hold the money.

Standing to my feet, I unlocked the safe and started loading thick stacks of $50,000 each straight into the bags.

Once I was done loading them, I took a step back and knew that I'd have a struggle getting out of the house. Shaking my head, I moved to pick out my outfit and decided on all-black once again. A pair of loose fitting black dress pants and a black long-sleeve shirt paired with my all-black Louboutins was my outfit of choice.

I still had a few hours before the meeting, but I just wanted everything to go smoothly. Sitting on my bed, I pulled out a bag of weed and swishers from the top drawer of my nightstand before I got back comfortable and rolled up. In silence, I laid back smoking my blunt full of cookies, trying to choke back the tears that were burning the back of my throat. Every moment that I had alone, I was overwhelmed with emotion and memories of Tristan.

"You were made for me."

Like my mind was playing tricks on me, I heard his voice loud and clear all too often.

Letting the weed take effect, I inhaled deeply holding in the smoke for as long as I could before releasing my breath, trying to take the bullshit off my mind. Usually, when I got high, it'd be with Tristan after we finished fucking or just when we had free-time to chill. Laying here smoking alone just didn't feel right.

In a trance, I thought about his presence and his touch as tears started to slide down my cheeks. The room was awkwardly silent until my stomach started rumbling and almost sounded like something was underneath my bed. With all that had been going on, I'd been forgetting to eat. It had apparently been one day too many 'cause the weed had woken my hunger up like a sleeping giant.

Getting up, I made my way to the kitchen to grab some snacks. I wasn't in the mood to eat anything big. I just wanted to kill these hunger pangs, so I made myself a quick turkey sandwich and grabbed a banana before returning to my room and devouring both of them like a starving child.

Today was Saturday, which meant that Tristan's funeral was only two-days away. Only two-days to mentally prepare myself to see the love of my life be forever lowered into the ground like he was nothing.

Sitting on the edge of my bed, tears fell from my eyes yet again. Grabbing T's pillow from behind me, I held it tightly as I rocked myself from side-to-side, trying to calm down. The weed, staying busy, and all this other bullshit were only temporary fixes. Anytime my high was gone or I had nothing to do, like a faucet, my tears just wouldn't stop pouring.

They say God puts his toughest battles on his strongest soldiers, so I knew that this too shall pass, but that didn't stop the pain from hitting me like a steel bat, reminding me that Tristan was gone, and he was never coming back.

After crying until I felt like I had no more tears left in me, I finally got my ass up and started getting ready for my meeting with Emiliano.

CHAPTER SIX

Riding down the freeway in Tristan's 2019 matte-black Continental Bentley GT, I headed to San Leandro where the meetup spot was. Reaching up, I turned the radio on and Bruno Mars ft. Cardi B's hit "Finesse" started blaring through my speakers. I needed something to calm my nerves, and music was always the perfect escape. Luckily, like me, Tristan loved to ride with his music blasting, so there was no need to adjust the volume.

Mentally, I was feeling better. I smoked another blunt before I left the house, and I was starting to feel like my mind was now in the right place for this meeting. I didn't know where Emiliano's head would be once he saw that I'd shown up alone, but I was hoping for the best.

Nearing the exit, I moved the car with precision to my right-hand lane and got off the freeway. T and Emiliano's meetup spot was an old warehouse out by the San Leandro Marina. Emiliano lived in Colombia, but he had no problem flying out here whenever there was money involved. I think he bought this warehouse just for business dealings 'cause he hadn't made a change to it in years.

Finally pulling into the warehouse's parking lot, my palms got a little sweaty. Emiliano had already arrived, and his men were guarding the perimeter of the old cement building.

After parking my car, a calming feeling swept over my body. It was almost like I could feel Tristan letting me know that he was watching over me.

Grabbing my purse and tossing my phone inside, I stepped out of the car with my head high and made my way to the trunk to retrieve the bags of money. Slightly struggling to carry both of the bags alone, all eyes were on me, and I knew everyone was wondering where the fuck Tristan was.

Walking up to the main door and entering the building, I found Emiliano sitting in a single chair. There were no others, so I assumed he planned to get right down to business.

"Felicia, it's so nice to see you again, mi belleza gruesa," he said as he got up to give me a quick hug and sat back down in his seat. Grabbing a cigar from his suit pocket, he held it to his mouth before one of his men came and lit it. Inhaling a thick cloud of smoke, he blew it out as if he was savoring the taste before turning his attention back to me. Raising his eyebrows in confusion, he looked suspiciously at only me standing before him.

"So, where is Tristan?" Looking towards the doors, I assumed he was waiting on him to come through them.

"Emiliano, have you seriously not heard?" I asked as I finally placed the heavy duffle bags I was carrying down on the floor.

"Heard what?" With a puzzled look on his tan face, he took another hit of his cigar.

"Someone killed Tristan four-days ago," I told him as I choked back the tears, keeping my head held high.

"What do you mean? How could this happen?"

"He was with Bleek, and someone caught him slipping. Bleek may not have been at fault, but he has been dealt with, and the mothafuckas who actually killed

T will be laid to rest just as easily. I'm here today in hopes that you'd be willing to continue doing business with me."

His laughter echoed loudly throughout the room catching me off guard.

"Morena, why would I continue doing business with you? This is a man's game. There is no place for a woman in this merciless business. You wouldn't even know what to do with the fifty kilos I had for Tristan." He looked at me like I was stupid for even suggesting such a thing.

"Actually, Emiliano, I know *exactly* what to do with those keys. Tristan kept me close for a reason. If needed, I know how to break those mothafuckas down and cook them, but that's not what I plan to do. I plan to sell each kilo still intact and make the maximum profit off of each one. This software I designed specifically for Tristan will allow me to view the most he's ever sold a key for," I told him as I pulled my iPad from out of my purse, pulling up the app so that I could show him.

Scrolling through the history, I found that Tristan sold his keys for $20,000 a piece, no lower. Showing Emiliano the setup of how T had been able to keep track of every transaction he'd ever made had him amazed.

"Can I see that?" he inquired. I nodded my head, passing the iPad over to him. "You designed this?" With a raised eyebrow, he looked up at me quickly before focusing back on the screen.

"Yep. Tristan used to come home sometimes high as hell and tell me that he had forgotten who all he'd picked up from that day, and, one night, my wheels just started turning. With Excel-like capabilities, it allows you to easily log who you've picked up from, how much product was given, and how much money you received in return. T wasn't big on giving out deals and shit, but if he did look out, and someone owed him something, all he'd have to do is press that negative dollar sign icon in the corner, and he could enter and view anything that was owed to him as well."

Walking around the warehouse still playing with the iPad, Emiliano was really intrigued, and I felt a glimmer of hope. I needed to get him to continue working with me so bad that I was nervous. My palms were sweaty, and all of his men were scaring the shit out of me.

"Could you possibly design something like this for me?" he asked, interrupting my thoughts as he came and stood in front of me before handing me the iPad back.

"Of course, I could. All I'd want in return is for you to consider continuing doing business with me. I know that the fact that I'm a woman is where your hesitation is coming from, but I assure you that I am not your *average* female. I know how to separate my feelings from business. I do not make any irrational decisions. I am a thinker. Growing up, I had four brothers who taught me so much, and, still to this day, it's hard to shake some of my old tomboy habits. I promise business with us will go just as smoothly as your business with Tristan did."

Awaiting his response, he just stared blankly at me like he was deeply contemplating his choice of words.

"…Felicia, I believe you are a very smart woman, and I have faith in you. What I can do is, assuming that's the full $500,000 that Tristan usually has for me, we can do the business deal today only. When next month comes around and it's time for our next meeting, if you do not have my money in full, there will be repercussions. One thing I do not play about, Felicia, is mi dinero. Woman or not, I will have to handle the situation accordingly, do you understand?"

"I understand," I said firmly.

With a look of uncertainty still in his eyes, Emiliano snapped his fingers, and one of his men came over and got the duffle bags. Bringing it up to the table, he started unpacking the stacks of money, loading it into a currency counter that they already had set up. Once the man was done, he looked over at Emiliano and nodded his head. In return, Emiliano did the same and again snapped his fingers, causing two other men headed out of the warehouse.

"Ahh, Felicia, I'm so sorry to hear about what has happened to Tristan. He was truly a great man." Coming close to me, he delicately placed his hand on me cheek as he spoke. "I'd hate to have to send you to join him." He threatened so nonchalantly that it sent chills up my spine as he pulled me in for a fake hug and started to walk out of the building.

"Uhh, where's my shit?" I asked confused.

"It's been taken care of," he said without looking back, and, one by one with their guns in hand, his men followed suit ready for whatever.

Walking slowly out of the warehouse, I followed behind them, watching as they all climbed into the two black Navigators they rode in and quickly pulled off. Shaking my head, I walked over to my car and popped the trunk. I had to give it to him, those motherfuckas were smooth. Filled to capacity were five duffle bags each containing ten bricks of pure heroin straight from Colombia. I marveled down at all the product in my trunk before closing it with the biggest grin on my face.

I'd gotten Emiliano to do business with me, and it felt good. Men were always underestimating me, but once I got to using this mouth God gave me, they had change of hearts almost instantly every time.

Making my way to the front of my car, my heels clicked loudly against the pavement before I eased behind the wheel. I was in such a good mood as I backed out of the parking space I was in with my music blasting. Reaching inside of the middle console, I pulled out a blunt and lit it before I turned out of the lot. There was one place Tristan kept all his product and only me, him, and Bleek knew about it.

After riding and finishing up the whole blunt, I finally pulled up to my destination. It was a little studio apartment out in Concord that Tristan had bought. He also used it as an office sometimes, but for the most part, it was only used to store work.

Finding a park right in front of the staircase, I got out to start unloading the bags. My feet were killing me with these damn heels on, and as I climbed the steps with two duffle bags on both of my arms, it damn-near felt like my ankles were going to break.

Once I made it to the top of the stairs, my big-ass was so outta breath I swore I needed an inhaler.

"Woo, I need to stop smoking," I said breathlessly as I pulled out my keys and entered the apartment.

Briefly setting the bags down, I took in the small place that looked like one of those display units that realtors showed when you were looking to lease an apartment. One thing that stood out though was the undeniable smell of Tristan's Armani Black. It lingered in the air like it was the one who lived here.

Shaking my head, I quickly picked the bags back up before walking over to the closet that sat near the bathroom. On the outside, it appeared to be just a regular hall closet, but we had it turned into a wall-to-wall safe.

After pulling open the regular door, I walked up to the tall metal one where a touchscreen pad sat, typed in the date of our anniversary, and put my index finger up to the fingerprint scanner. There was a loud unlocking sound before I was able to turn the knob and pull the door open. Setting the bags down inside, I then stepped out of the closet to take my heels off. I didn't have any socks or anything else to put on, but, at this point, I didn't give a fuck. My dawgs were howling.

Leaning up against the wall, I pulled my shoes off and felt instant relief. I swear if I could've just worn sneakers all the time, that'd be fine with me. My mother was always so big on me acting and dressing like a lady though that heels and other girly shit just started to come naturally to me I got older.

As I unloaded more bags, I just shook my head at the thought of my mama's prissy-ass. I tried to avoid her at all costs because she always had an opinion that nobody wanted to hear. She was always nitpicking at everything I did, and the shit drove me crazy.

"Felicia, cross your legs. Felicia, sit up straight. Sweatpants? Really, Felicia? Did you just roll out of bed?" I thought to myself as I mimicked her voice.

When I was younger, I used to run around outside with my brothers, and it killed her. She'd buy all these dolls and a bunch of clothes and accessories to go with them, but I didn't care about that shit. I just wanted to be with my brothers. As we got older though, one by one, they all started to go off to college and created lives of their own, so it was just me and my younger brother who was honestly an afterthought being six-years younger than me, leaving my mom to hold me up to this sky-high standard that I knew I could never meet. I would never be good enough in her eyes, but I didn't let that shit bother me. Even now, in all of my success, she always had so much to say on what *else* I could be doing. I hated that shit, so I just kept my distance.

Running back down the stairs, I grabbed the last bag before I closed my trunk and ran barefoot back up the concrete stairs. It was nearing sunset, and there was a cool breeze in the air that just made me want to go sit outside and read.

Once again, a little winded I walked into the studio and closed the door behind me. Placing the bag on the floor, I unzipped it and saw that there were also two kilos of coke inside this bag. As far as I knew, Tristan only dealt with black, but I mean, I wasn't mad. It was all money.

For the H, he would usually bring a fiend with him and have them test the product, but he'd been fucking with Emiliano for so long that he no longer needed a tester. Their relationship was a loyal one but being as though this was a new business agreement, I knew I couldn't expect the same.

Getting down on my knees, I pulled the bag in front of me and cut a small hole inside one of the keys with my nail. Using my pinky finger, I dug deep inside the powder. With the white residue coating my finger, I quickly rubbed it on my gums, trying to make sure this shit was legit. I didn't even know how it was supposed to feel, but, shit…I knew I needed to be feeling *something*.

Being that Emiliano was skeptical to fuck with me in the first place, I figured he might try to play me, but when my whole mouth instantly started to get numb, I knew that this shit was nothing to play with. I'd only seen Tristan do this shit. I've never actually tried it before, and I was already regretting it. My mouth started to get really dry, and my ass was now paranoid like someone had seen me with all these drugs.

Picking up the bag, I briskly walked back to the safe before I slammed it shut and hurried to relock it. After closing the closet door, I swore I thought I'd heard another door slam shut, causing my eyes to almost pop out my head as I nervously looked around the apartment.

You're trippin', bitch, I thought in my head but laughed out loud.

Still laughing to myself, I reached in my purse for my phone and called Mikel.

"What you want, hoe?" he answered playfully.

"*Bestiieeeee,*" I said as I pressed my mouth against the phone. I was starting to feel numb all over.

"Bitch, I know you ain't drunk. Oh, my god, this shit finna turn you into an alcoholic. Nah, bitch, I'm not having it, I'm coming over for an intervention," he said seriously, causing me to bust out laughing extra loud.

"Nigga, you dumb. I ain't drunk. I'm just high as fuck, bestie," I told him as I sat on the floor, poking my face with the phone to my ear.

"*Mmm, mm, mm,* bitch, high off what? You acting stupid as I don't know what the fuck." He was clearly irritated.

"That's angel dust, homes," I said, mimicking Hector from *Friday* as I once again started cracking up.

"Oh, hell no, I'm on my way," he quickly said before he ended the call.

"I'm not even at home, mothafucka!" I yelled into the phone, now talking to myself.

As I got up from the floor, I felt so lightweight as I walked across the carpet and grabbed my heels before I left out the apartment. I was feeling so high I swear the concrete felt like pillows as I held onto the railing and walked down the steps.

The whole way back to my apartment, I felt so good that I barely remembered my ride there. All I knew was that I felt so carefree.

I pulled into my driveway just as Mikel was coming up the street, and I couldn't help but laugh to myself.

Getting out, I smiled as I watched him rush to park his car and hop out with the quickness.

"Uh, uh, bitch, get yo' ass in the house," he said with a scolding tone as he rounded his car, speed-walking over to me.

I was laughing so hard at his ass that my stomach started to hurt. Wearing a pair of turquoise skinny jeans and a white tight-fitting shirt with a black moto jacket and knee-high leather boots to match, Mikel swore he was somebody's mama. His smooth milk chocolate skin was blemish-free, and his usually brightly-colored short fade was jet-black today.

"Don't start with me, bitch!" I said still barefoot as we entered the house together.

"Now, what the hell is going on?" he asked, grilling me as soon as the door was locked behind us.

"I had to go meet with T's connect today. I needed to convince him to continue doing business with me."

"Did he agree?" Mikel asked as we took a seat on my plush sectional.

"Bitch, I wouldn't be high for nothing. I had to make sure his ass wasn't tryna play me," I said with a serious face as Mikel started cracking up.

"What you thought he sold you flour or something?" he asked, dying laughing.

"You laughing but you never fucking know."

"Bitch, that coca just got you paranoid. He wouldn't do you like that."

"Don't play like you don't know me…trust is *earned,* not given," I told him as I got up to go get a water from out the fridge.

"Don't be rude, hoe; get me one too," I heard him shout from the couch right before I was about to close the refrigerator door, "So, is everything set for the funeral?"

Making my way back to the living room, I handed him the water before sitting Indian-style next to him.

"Yeah, I'm assuming so. I told Mama C that she could just handle all that shit, and I'll take care of the financial part. I want her to be able to lay her child to rest without me accidently stepping on her toes," I told him as I brought the bottle of water to my lips and started guzzling it down.

"Thirsty-ass hoe," Mikel sneered playfully as he rolled his eyes, "Where's the weed, bitch? Let's smoke." Playfully hitting me in the back of my head, he made his way to my room sniffing loudly trying to find the weed.

CHAPTER SEVEN

My whole day yesterday was pretty much a big blur. From the time Kel and I woke up, we were drinking and smoking non-fucking-stop, and my silly-ass tried that coke. I was having a hangover times ten and felt queasy as fuck. My head was pounding, and the realization that I had to bury my fiancé today hit me once again like a ton of bricks. I was feeling so numb yesterday, only to wake up with tears already streaming down my face today.

Sitting up in the bed, I looked around the room that Tristan and I used to share together and knew that I couldn't stay in this house anymore. There were just too many memories of T everywhere I turned, and I couldn't deal with it. With tears still coming down my face, I made my way over to his closet before grabbing one of the hoodies he had left on the floor. Picking it up, I held it tightly in my arms before my sobs became uncontrollable. Curling up on the floor, there I laid feeling like my heart had been ripped out of my chest.

"Fe?" Entering the closet and finding me on the floor the way I was, Mikel's expression quickly saddened from the big grin that was plastered on his face before.

Getting down on the floor with me, he pulled me up slightly and laid me on his lap as he gently stroked my hair. We didn't even speak to each other. For a whole hour, we just sat there and waited until I felt like I could finally get up.

Being the first to stand, I held my hand out so that I could help Mikel up before heading to get in the shower.

Now, in front of my full-length mirror smoking a blunt, I didn't feel better. Wearing a two-piece all-black pants suit with a matching pair of Christian Louboutin booties, I looked well put together on the outside, but, inside, I felt like I was the one dying. Looking at my reflection in the mirror, I toyed with my hair in disgust just as Mikel walked back in the room. He was looking fly in his tux and dress shoes. All he needed was for me to fix his tie. Mikel never wore stuff like this though, so to see him wearing this shit and I didn't have to beat him into it brought a slight smile to my face.

"Yo' ass gon' fuck around and catch some pussy tonight. You better put on some hoop earrings or something," I joked as I approached him and started adjusting his tie.

"Ugh, a bitch would want *not* to try me. The fuck can a pussy do fa me? Not a mothafucking thing…"

Chuckling to myself, I finished his tie before turning back around to face the mirror and sighed.

"Your hair looks fine, Felicia. Don't start that shit," he said, referring to my insecure rants. I couldn't help myself though. I just wanted everything to be perfect, but the fact of the matter was that nothing would be. Today would be a day that I would never forget, so If I looked fat or my hair was fucked up, I honestly didn't care, but I would remember.

My heart was being put into the ground today, and, from this day forth, I knew that nothing would ever be the same again.

Hearing my phone ringing from the kitchen counter, I knew that it was our car service letting us know that they had arrived. Taking a deep breath in and blowing it out, I tried to calm my nerves, but I knew that nothing would be able to stop my tears once they started again.

Mama C went all out for her only baby boy, and no matter what the price was, whatever she wanted, I was happy to oblige. I didn't think she'd be able to plan everything in such a short amount of time, but she proved me wrong. Everything was immaculate, from his gold encrusted casket down to the custom-made black and gold Ferragamos that adorned his feet.

With heavy hearts, Mikel and I rode to the funeral home smoking blunt after blunt. The driver had to roll the divider up. I'm sure he couldn't wait for us to get out of his car.

When we finally arrived in front of Fouché's, there were already people starting to arrive. I saw a few familiar faces, but everyone held their heads down and wore sad expressions as they filed inside. Although, many men envied Tristan and even hated him, the love people had for him outweighed anything else.

Growing up in Oakland, Tristan experienced the struggle firsthand. He knew how it felt to have to wear the same shit from the last school year into the new one. He knew how it felt to not have any presents on Christmas or no food on Thanksgiving. So, any chance he got, he was giving back to the young boys in the hood, making sure they had school supplies and school clothes. He'd even go as far as walking some of the kids home to make sure they had food, and that they were straight. Tristan's heart was so big, and I knew that he would truly be missed.

Grabbing my clutch, I followed behind Mikel as we exited the car and walked hand-in-hand up to the entrance. With my hair down in loose curls and big Gucci frames covering my eyes, you almost couldn't tell who I was. Those who knew both me and Tristan though could spot my ass from a mile away because of my voluptuous figure.

As we entered the building, a bunch of people were already seated in the pews shedding tears silently and talking about memories they shared with T. All of the men on his payroll and people he fucked with were in attendance, and Tupac's "Heaven for a G" was playing softly throughout the room.

I could already feel that familiar burning feeling in the back of my throat letting me know that I wouldn't be able to hold my tears back much longer. The energy in here was one that would make even the hardest nigga shed a tear. Everyone was seriously heartbroken by Tristan's death. In the midst of everything though, it felt good to know that he'd left such an impact on so many people.

Finally making it to the front row, I spotted Mama C who looked beautiful despite the tears that were effortlessly sliding down her face. When she looked up and saw me, a weird expression came over her face as she quickly stood up and hurried to approach me. Pulling me in for a hug, she whispered in my ear.

"Today is about Tristan. Please, don't start no drama. I don't know all the details...they just showed up at my house last night."

I was so confused as to what the hell she was talking about until she pulled away from me and stepped to the side. There sat a light-skinned woman sitting next to a little girl. The girl couldn't've been no older than 2-years-old, and as I stared at her a little longer...my heart started rapidly beating in my chest.

It can't be. She can't...is this shit really happening to me right now?

So many thoughts were racing through my mind, but as I looked from the little girl who was the spitting image of my fiancé back up to her mama who had a smug-ass grin on her face, the only thing running through my mind was why didn't I put my fucking nine in my purse.

As if he could read my mind, Mikel grabbed my arm and pulled me down the aisle and back out of the building. I did my best to stay respectful while we were inside, but once we were out, I turned the fuck up.

"Did you see that shit? Did you see that mothafuckin' little girl? How the fuck and where the fuck did that lil' bitch come from? And, who the fuck do that Alf-looking-ass bitch think she is?! Is she serious? Ugly-ass hoe lucky as fuck I left my shit at home 'cause we would've been burying *two* mothafuckas in there." Moving my hand with each word I spoke, I was being so animated, but I didn't give a fuck. I was heated.

"I saw, but, Fe, you got to calm down."

"Did this mothafucka Tristan really have the audacity to have a baby on me? Is this nigga serious? I feel like slapping the shit out his dumbass. Matter fact…" Turning on my heels, I headed back inside when Mikel roughly grabbed my arm, pulling me back.

"Look, bitch, ya' nigga cheated on you and had a baby," he said, saying the shit as if it meant nothing, "I know this shit hurts, but he's dead, Fe. You can't spaz on a dead man, and you can't disrespect him like that, not here. You wanna see wassup with 'ol girl we can see about her ass later, but right now, we gotta go lay yo' man to rest, a man who loved you and *only* you. Don't let this broad get you all razzle dazzled. Keep it cute, and we'll handle all the bullshit later." Still holding onto my arm, Mikel always knew exactly what to say.

Taking a deep breath in through my nose and then blowing it out through my mouth, I calmed my nerves a bit as Kel finally released his grip on my arm.

Placing my glasses back on my face, I flipped my hair over my shoulder before grabbing Mikel's hand and re-entering the building.

The service was just about to start as we made our way to our seats. The shady guy I met when I came here with Mama C took the podium, and the whole room became silent.

"Family and friends, I want to welcome you today to this special service in memory and in celebration of the life of young Tristan Combs. We gather here, no doubt, with many mixed emotions, feelings of sadness and sorrow over the loss of a loved one, a friend, a son, and a fiancé, but, also, we gather here today with feelings of joy, knowing that Tristan is now with our Father in paradise."

As soon as he said Tristan's name, tears immediately began to slide down my face as I finally looked at his casket. I'd been avoiding eye contact with it because I knew that once I saw him I wouldn't be able to stop my tears. They were flowing so rapidly as I half-listened to this janky pastor we had up there. I should've honestly just spoken up when I had the chance because this cat really just rubbed me the wrong way.

Almost feeling like I was unable to breathe from crying so hard, I felt Kel grip my hand tighter, trying to let me know that it was gonna be okay. Taking a deep breath, I watched as Mama C made her way up to the podium trying to control her own tears as well. She recounted memories of Tristan running butt naked through her house, the day he graduated from high school, and the day she brought him into this world. No longer able to control her tears, she got weak in the knees as the funeral director hurried over to assist her. The whole room was now in tears as he took his spot back at the podium.

"Shall we pray?" he asked before clearing his throat, "Lord of Heaven and Creator of all things, we thank you for the gift of life. Not only for the gift of life here on Earth but also the promise of eternal life that comes only through Jesus, your son. You are the Lord, and we thank you for watching over each and every one of us. We pray for our time together this afternoon during this service. We pray that it would be honoring to you and honoring to Tristan. During this time of grief and pain, we ask that you bring comfort, peace, and your presence into all of our lives as we need you now more than ever, Lord. Amen."

Boom!

With the last word spoken, the door to the funeral home was roughly kicked open, and a barrage of bullets started flying around us. With our instincts instantly kicking in, Mikel and I both hit the floor, ducking down in front of our seats. Quickly looking up, I saw that the little girl from earlier was screaming, still sitting in her seat. Reaching my arm up, I hurried to pull her down with us before noticing that her mom was slumped.

One thing off my to-do list, I thought heartlessly to myself.

I could hear Jacari and some of the other men firing back, but I couldn't see through the haze of the gunfire. Once the bullets stopped, Jacari and his boys sprinted outside still letting off shots at the unknown gunmen.

Once the shots finally ceased, the room fell silent, and I knew that it was okay for us to get up. Using the seat as leverage, I picked myself up before helping the little girl do the same. Before she could see that her mother had a bullet wound to the back of her head, I hurried to shield her, pulling her into my stomach as we walked towards the exit.

"Mama C?!" I nervously called out because, as I looked around the room, I didn't see her anywhere.

"Over here, Felicia," I heard her say but didn't know where her voice was coming from.

Passing the baby to Mikel, I backtracked, calling out to her again until I found her. She was on the floor behind the pew.

"I think my ankle is broken. Why would anyone do something like this, Felicia?" she sobbed uncontrollably as I helped her up and out of the building as best as I could.

Looking around the room, there was glass strewn about, seats knocked over, and bullet holes all along the side of Tristan's casket. Now crying even harder, everyone was filing out of the building in confusion. Me on the other hand, I was walking out the room with one thing on my mind. Why were these niggas still coming so hard? With Tristan dead, you'd think they'd be trying to lay low, but these fools seemed like they had no plan on stopping anytime soon.

After making sure Mama C and the little girl got into a car safely, I made my way over to Mikel fuming.

"We got to get a handle on this shit," I told him as tears of anger finally fell from my eyes.

CHAPTER EIGHT

Now sitting in my living room next to Mikel as we took turns sipping a pint of Hennessy, all that was on my mind was revenge. Even though I just found out that Tristan possibly had a baby on me, that did nothing to change the love I had for him. I couldn't believe that some mothafuckas were bold enough to shoot up his funeral like it was nothing. Anger filled my veins as I thought about all the bullet holes in his casket.

"Fuck! I swear to God I'm ready to just lay some shit down." Jumping up from the couch with the bottle of Henny still in hand, I made my fingers into a fake gun and aimed it at Kel's head.

"A'ight now, killa, sit yo' dumbass down." His ass was crackin' up, but I was dead-ass. I wanted somebody to bleed like they left my baby bleeding. I wanted whoever these mothafuckas were to pay for taking my love away from me.

"I'm serious, bitch!" I said, lightly pushing him back before I sat back down next to him, "I gotta figure out who these mothafuckas are. We just need one lead."

"Well, whoever they are, they're making sure to stay extra lowkey. I ain't heard shit 'bout no new niggas in the Bay, and you know I stay up on *all* the tea," he said before taking another swig from the bottle.

Being the owner of one of the hottest hair salons in the City, Mikel wasn't lying. Any tea you needed to know on anybody, you could find out in that messy-ass shop. That's why I was glad that Kel was my bestie. I got the front door treatment drama-free.

"Man, somebody gotta know something about theses niggas," I said just as my phone started ringing in my purse. It was Jacari.

"Ay, Fe, I got some news, ma," he said as if he could read my mind.

"A'ight, lay it down," I told him, slightly smiling.

"After that shit went down earlier, we all was hot, looking for answers, and you ain't gon' believe what I stumbled on."

Taking a seat back on the couch, I switched the phone to speaker as Mikel and I both listened intently.

"So, these mothafuckas been in plain sight, just ain't nobody been looking for them. I asked my girl Tamia who works at City Nights, this club that be yanking in the City."

"I know about City Nights, Cari," I told him as I chuckled lightly.

"Anyway, I asked her if any new niggas had been sliding through big spending, acting like they wit' it. She ain't even have to think twice about the shit. Like, she knew exactly what I was talking 'bout already off that alone. But, to make sure we was talking 'bout the same nigga, I had her describe the one who looked like he was in charge and *boom!* I found the nigga we looking for. The nigga's real name is Josiah, but on the streets they callin him 'Murder Joe.' Tamia say she's been to the nigga's crib before, and she's been hearing them niggas boast about taking down the hottest nigga in the Bay. It's him fa sho…how you wanna handle this shit?"

When that last question came out his mouth, my heart dropped to the bottom of my stomach as I nervously looked at Mikel. I didn't want to be irrational. Tristan

65

always told me that acting on impulse was most these niggas' biggest downfall. I needed to move smart and think before I acted off my emotions.

"I'ma hit you in the morning and let you know what the move is. Thank you for looking out though. I owe you big for this."

"You know I fucked with T the long way. None of us ain't gon' sleep right 'til them niggas in the dirt. If you want us to handle it, just say the word. I'll holla at 'chu in the a.m. though."

After hanging up the phone and setting it down beside me, I fell back into my plush couch pillows deep in thought. Suddenly, it felt like the weight of the world was now on my shoulders, and we didn't even get to lay Tristan to rest peacefully yet. Tomorrow, we would be meeting at his gravesite to finally lay my baby to rest, but that wouldn't stop the bullshit from coming. I knew that this shit needed to be handled, but we needed a plan.

Kel and I used to run with these two bitches Nalia and Talia. They were with the shit and bad as fuck. If I could get them close to this Josiah mothafucka, that would put everything in motion for us to really get at his ass.

"Kel, you remember them crazy-ass twins from college? Dark skin and *really* crazy as hell?" I asked, sitting down next to him. His ass had been extra quiet, just letting me think.

"Yeah, I remember them hoes. They always had a hammer on them and stayed playin' and shit. What about them bitches?" he asked, clearly uninterested.

"Well, I'm finna hit them up, so we can put they ass on a line like bait to reel this nigga Josiah in and rock his ass right to sleep," I said, punching my hand for emphasis.

"Brah, sometimes, I swear you more of a nigga than me." Shaking his head, he rolled his eyes while laughing to himself, and I couldn't help but laugh with him.

When I was younger, my brothers would say I was supposed to be a boy anyway. I had four big brothers, and they were hoping to continue the trend, but they got stuck with me. Growing up, they had me lifting weights, catching bugs, and climbing trees. Anywhere they were, I wanted to be, but my mama wasn't having that. When we were home, it was one thing, but when they went to go hang out with their friends, I was always left hanging. I'd be sitting on my front porch for as long as I could, waiting for them to come home.

Sitting here thinking about my brothers made me realize that I hadn't called them or my mother in a few months. I had gotten so wrapped up in my own life that I'd been forgetting to check on them.

"Bitch, if you don't pass the mothafuckin Henny back dis way, I'm finna bop yo' shit."

Breaking me from my thoughts with his pettiness, Mikel had his head tilted to the side and his fists up causing me to crack up laughing.

"Ain't shit funny, bitch…sitting over there looking like *That's So Raven* and shit, fuck outta here," he said playfully while snatching the bottle from my hand.

"Fuck you! I'm finna go see if I can find the twins' number and roll up…come on."

Getting up from my tan plush couch, I walked barefoot across the floor to my bedroom smiling. These past couple weeks had been hectic but being with my best friend truly made everything feel like it was going to be okay.

"So, after the burial ceremony tomorrow, you officially gon' be the head of all of Tristan's businesses. You sure you really want this shit?"

Sitting down on my bed bringing a small trashcan in front of me, I started breaking down a swisher as I thought.

"Now, you know I ain't one to backdown from a challenge. I know all these niggas thinking I'm gon' be in over my head and all that bullshit but watch how we finna get this money though."

Getting hype, Kel instantly held his hand out so we could slap fives.

"Okay, bitch…let's get this mothafuckin' money then, Tony!" he said, mimicking Al Pacino's voice from *Scarface.*

Our silly asses spent the rest of the night smoking big blunts and ended up making a store run for another bottle. When morning came, and my alarm started going off, we both were moaning and groaning loud as hell 'cause neither of us wanted to get up but knew we had to. Besides, the sun was shining super bright through my window, almost blinding us anyway.

Literally rolling my ass out of the king-size bed, I stumbled over to my bathroom and held myself up with the counter before looking at myself in the mirror. I was a hot-ass mess.

"Kel, get yo' ass up, bitch! We got an hour to get ready," I shouted out the door before walking over to my glass shower and turning it on all the way hot, hoping it would warm up quicker.

"Bitch, you finna have to bury this nigga yo'self 'cause I ain't coming."

Dramatically rolling off the bed onto the floor, his ass was gettin' on my nerves.

Walking over to him, I playfully acted like I was kicking him in his side before trying to pull him off the floor. I got half his body off the ground before I thought about it and let his ass go, making him hit his head as he dropped.

"Bitch, you better be lucky you got this fluffy-ass carpet or else I'd be all over yo' ass right now fucking you up."

Quickly sitting up on his elbows, he was looking at me like he really wanted to beat my ass.

Dying laughing, I walked back into my bathroom 'cause the steam was now rapidly filling my bedroom, and I needed to turn the heat down.

Once I got it to the perfect temp, which wasn't too far from all the way hot, I admired my body in the mirror and blew myself a kiss.

Big and beautiful, baby, I thought to myself as I climbed inside.

After taking care of my hygiene, I threw on some black slacks with a white long-sleeved blouse and paired it with a black and white blazer. Always needing to make sure I looked my best, I walked over to my full-length mirror and gave myself the once over. Looking at the time, we now had only twenty-minutes to get to the burial site. Luckily, Mikel was throwing on his clothes too.

Thankfully, I wasn't too drunk last night to put on my bonnet, so my edges were still laid. Pulling it off, I brushed my hair down and was good to go.

The whole ride to the gravesite was silent. I didn't have anything to say, and I knew Mikel, who always had something to say, was just tryna give me time to get my thoughts together.

Pulling up alongside the curb, I hesitantly got out as I looked around at all the plaques lined one after the other.

I'd always been good at painting on a face when inside I was really a mess. Trying to, this time though, was truly challenging as I felt my breath get caught in my throat. Finally willing my feet to move away from the car, I proceeded up the eerie pathway. My heels were clicking loudly against the pavement only adding to my anxiety…until we reached the grass where I grabbed Mikel's hand for support because, all of a sudden, my knees felt weak.

We saw Fouché and Mama C plus the little girl from the funeral standing around a brand-new casket and hurried to head that way because they looked like they were waiting on us.

"Sorry, if we're a little late, you guys," I said to everyone as I linked arms with Mikel. The wind seemed to be blowing stronger than usual in Oakland today.

"It's fine, baby…you're here now." Holding the little girl close, Mama C shook her head at me in understanding.

"Well, since everyone's here, I guess we can get started. Did anyone have a few words they wanted to say before I begin?" Fouché asked, standing in front of Tristan's casket.

"Yeah, I got something to ask actually. Where the fuck did you disappear to when everything was going down at *your* funeral home?"

All eyes were now on him because I was sure everyone else was wondering the same thing.

"Bullets were flying everywhere, and you all expected me to stick around?" Cutting his eyes at me, this fool had the nerve to look like he now had an attitude.

"A'ight, let's just get this over with. Tristan has waited too long to finally rest peacefully." I was so ready to get away from this clown.

*****

Sitting in the grass next to Tristan's headstone, tears were streaming down my face as I looked at the spot where they covered his casket with dirt. I'd been sitting here for hours, and I still wasn't ready to leave yet.

Everything was fine until I saw them lower him into the ground. It felt like they were taking something from me, and I just started spazzing on everybody. How could everyone be so calm about this? How could they just leave him so easily?

Mama C was so adamant about taking care of that little girl, but she didn't even know if she was Tristan's. There hadn't been no fuckin' DNA test, and how the fuck you gon' get DNA from a dead man anyway? Acting like she cared more about that brat than she did her own child.

Finally standing up from the grass, I wiped my face, but more tears immediately fell again.

"Them mothafuckas are going to die slow, my love…I promise you. Rest easy."

Placing a kiss on his headstone, I finally found the courage to get up and leave the cemetery. Mikel was waiting for me in the car. By now, I was surprised that he hadn't left my ass.

CHAPTER NINE

The sound of my phone ringing caused me to jump out of my sleep. Grabbing it from off the nightstand, I blindly answered without knowing who it was.

"You playing with the big boys now, bitch," the person said and then ended the call.

Whoever the fuck it was had a deep-ass voice that, I'm guessing, was supposed to be intimidating, but no man pumped fear in my heart.

Swinging my legs over the side of my bed, I prepared to get up when my phone started ringing once again.

"Hey, Jacari…good morning," I spoke as I stretched.

"It is not a good fucking morning, Felicia. Somebody just hit two of our spots in the Town, and we've been losing our customers left and fucking right. You told everybody to put shit on hold, and that only put shit in motion for this nigga Josiah and his niggas to move in and start taking over our territory. Fe, if you're in over yo' head, just let me know, ma, and I'll help you, but this shit right here gon' fuck around and leave you as a one-woman team," he spoke honestly.

"Fuck! I was just tryna…"

"Look, I know what you was tryna do, but this dope shit don't stop for nobody. Ya' whole shit will crumble if you move like that."

"Okay, so, look…get the word out to get shit back moving. I know for a fact them clowns don't have better product than us, so I'm sure y'all shouldn't have no problems getting y'all clientele back. Now about the spots that got hit, I'ma handle that shit too. Don't even trip. I just want to thank you for lookin' out," I told him with sincerity.

"Don't thank me, just reciprocate the loyalty. I'll holla at you later, Fe," he replied before hanging up.

"Damn, bitch! You ain't see me sleeping with yo' loud-mouth-ass?" Kel said, causing me to jump. I forgot his ass was even here.

"Go home, Roger!" I mocked and threw a pillow at him.

Getting up from my bed, I moved over to my computer, so that I could check my emails from work. There were a bunch from people sending their condolences and one from Rachel. She was telling me that she was so sorry for my loss but that I needed to get back to work before she had to kill one of them white folks. I couldn't help but smile as I read it because I missed her ass.

There were a few other emails from some of my clients requesting updates or paperwork, and that let me know that I needed to return to work sooner rather than later.

As I prepared to go handle my hygiene, my phone chimed with an incoming message; it was the twins. They agreed to meet with me and have lunch today.

Clinching the phone in my hands, I shuddered with excitement. For the right price, I knew that they'd be down for whatever, and that meant I was one step closer to Josiah.

After showering, I stood in front of my mirror wand-curling my hair as Mikel sat on the counter passing me a blunt.

"So, you sure about fucking with these hoes, right? I remember how crazy they asses used to be, and we definitely don't need no unwanted attention right now."

"I'm sure. I remember how they were too, and I know they probably thinking I'm still that nonchalant, laidback Felicia, but they gon' be in for a rude awakening if they try to play me. I'll push one of them bitches' wigs back quicker than the thought of them crossing me would even come to mind."

Shrugging my shoulders, I made a mental note to keep my nine on me wherever I went from now on.

"Yeah, okay, Fe, please, just don't let all this shit change you."

Hopping down from the counter, he moved behind me to help me with the back of my hair.

"Don't be tryna get all sentimental and shit. Nigga, you know I would never switch up on you, so kill that noise," I joked as he rolled his eyes trying not to smile.

"Whatever, bitch, let's go."

Finishing up the last curl, Mikel put the blunt out as I played with my hair, adding volume to my curls and a faux bang. I just brought some of my hair over my face before securing it with a bobby pin.

Grabbing my favorite plum-colored MAC lipstick, I dropped it in my black and gray Fendi clutch, and we were out the door.

No matter how much money I made, I would never be too good to eat at Fridays. Their appetizers and drinks were just as good if not better than the fancy upscale places, so fuck it…that's where I told the twins to meet us.

Finally pulling in front of the restaurant, I put yet another blunt we'd been smoking out and wasted no time climbing out of my car. On our way inside, I looked over at Mikel and patted my clutch letting him know we wasn't 'bout to play no games with these hoes.

As we entered the building, a short white girl with a smile that was way too wide greeted us.

"Table for two?" she asked, grabbing two menus.

Looking around the restaurant, I spotted the twins over at the bar, so I held my hand up, stopping her.

"I think we're just gonna have a seat at the bar," I told her as I nudged Mikel and nodded to where they were seated.

"Oh, well, in that case, just grab a seat wherever you'd like," she told us after putting the menus back and holding her hand out in the direction of the bar.

As we maneuvered through the tables, making our way over to the twins, I took a deep breath and put my gameface on. These two were nothing to play with...but neither was I.

"OMG, Fe, Mikel, it has been way too long!" Nalia squealed, being the first to stand up and hug me.

"Oh, my god, I know. Look at you!" I exclaimed as we pulled away from our embrace. She looked so different, but I couldn't put my finger on what it was. However, when she turned around to take her seat, my curiosity vanished. They definitely had some work done. The twins I remembered used to be thick but nothing like this. In my opinion, it was a bit much, but their waists were snatched, and if they liked it...hey, I loved it.

"Hey, Fe," Talia said, breaking me from my thoughts and bringing me in for a quick hug as well.

After we all took our seats, I flagged the bartender over, so we could get some drinks started. I did want to get right down to business, but I also wanted to catch up with my girls. With everything that had been going on lately, any excuse to let my hair down, I was taking it.

"Alright, y'all already know…spill it. Where the hell y'all been, and what y'all been up to?" I asked once everyone had ordered.

"Well, recently, we were just out in ATL doing a music video for Gucci Mane, but, bitch, we be all over. We secure the bag by any means. What y'all been up to though? Fe, you look like you've been doing real well. I see them red bottoms, hoe," Nalia joked just as our drinks arrived.

"Well, after college, y'all know me, I just kept my head in the books, and, now, I'm president of my company. Life has been good," I said with pride.

"And, what about that fine-ass man of yours we be seeing on Instagram? How's he?" Talia asked a little too eager, but I didn't think too much into it.

Putting my head down, I just couldn't bring myself to say that he died. His death was like a fresh wound that had yet to start healing.

"He passed away, y'all," Mikel whispered, and I could instantly see the look of pity that came over their faces.

"Fe, we are so sorry, girl. We had no idea," Talia said sincerely as she placed her hand over mine.

"It's coo…y'all know me. I was built Ford tough; this ain't gon' break me. I put that on the hood I'm good. I'm good," I joked as I sang along to YG's song, trying to lighten the mood.

We ended up ordering a bunch of appetizers and a few more drinks as we got each other all caught up on what had been going on in our lives. Now, full, tipsy, and ready smoke, I had to tell them the real reason why I'd asked them to meet me here.

"Alright, so before we part ways, I have a proposition for you guys."

"Okay, bitch, we were waiting. I mean, don't get me wrong, we missed you and all, but I knew it had to be something for you to just hit us up out the blue," Talia said, looking over at her sister.

"Well, I'm trying to find the dudes who murdered my fiancé. After hacking into OPD's internal servers, I was able to get a picture of the guy, and I now know where we can find him. I wanna move smart, and I could really use y'all's help," I spoke honestly.

"So, wait a minute...you did what? Nah, never mind, spare me the details," Talia chuckled

"Yo' ass ain't changed a bit. You still that same nerdy-ass Fe, but you know we got you. Whatever you need, just let us know."

"And, y'all know money ain't a thing, so I'm going to for sure look out for y'all. When I get all the details on where this nigga finna be at next, I'ma hit you up and give y'all instructions from there," I told them as I glanced over at Mikel who was being unusually quiet.

"A'ight, but before you go, I gotta question. Can you hack my nigga's Facebook? I swear his dog-ass is cheating, but I can't get no evidence. The nigga stay on point." Nalia was grinning, and I could tell she was tipsy as hell.

"Bitch, call me in the morning. I'll see what I can do," I laughed, "But, it was so good catching up with y'all. We all need to go out soon or something."

Getting up from our seats, I pulled down my blazer as we all prepared to leave. Grabbing the bill, I placed two $100 bills inside as everyone waited on me, and we proceeded out the door. The restaurant was facing towards the street, and as we exited, the cars riding by made the impact of the wind crazy. My hair was blowing everywhere as we all said our final goodbyes.

It was now dark outside, but we were all tipsy and feeling good as we stood outside the restaurant laughing before we finally parted ways. Still giggling, Mikel and I waved bye to the twins before we made our way back to my car. Looking around the parking lot, I briefly searched my surroundings before opening my door and climbing inside. With all the bullshit going on, I had to stay on my toes 'cause I never knew who could be lurking in the shadows.

CHAPTER TEN

With my hair up in a tight bun, I was riding passenger as Mikel pushed my silver 2019 Range Rover down the 680 freeway. Wearing some dark gray sweatpants with a matching pullover hoodie, holding my Glock eighteen, I marveled at the matte-black finish as I smiled to myself. It had the look of a regular pistol but was fully automatic and would let off twenty-rounds in under thirty-seconds.

We were on our way to meet with a consultant from a new security firm I was looking into. After putting some thought to it, I realized that maybe Kel and my nine would no longer be enough. I'd just taken over Tristan's position, and I didn't know what these niggas were gonna try next. I knew for sure that they were pussies, but by no means was I going to underestimate them.

SATS Security was an independent security firm that the twins had hooked us up with. When we talked earlier this morning, they recommended them with no hesitation. They apparently knew the owners and trusted them to the fullest.

As the sun shined brightly through the windshield, I was definitely feeling a little skeptical, but it was whatever at this point.

Exiting off the freeway, the GPS told us to stay right off the Broadway exit, and I exhaled a little. The place was in Downtown Oakland, so they obviously had to be legit.

As we rode by the building that our meeting was in, heading to the parking garage, all my worries were settled. The sun was shining brightly off the huge office building, and all I wondered if it was all theirs.

After parking, we followed signs for the elevators to make our way inside.

Outside the parking garage, the sidewalk was filled with a bunch of people walking both past and towards us. The cool air instantly hit my skin and paired with the warmth of the sun; the weather was perfect today. Cars were whizzing up and down the crowded roads as we made it to the building and entered the lobby. A slender brown-skinned woman wearing an all-black pants suit greeted us from the front desk with a pretty white smile.

"Welcome to 600 Broadway, how can I help you?" she spoke as she batted her long eyelashes.

"We have a meeting with Kateira from SATS Security," I said as I rested my body against the counter, turning around to look at the beautiful day outside.

"Okay, I'll just need to see your IDs," I heard her say from behind me.

Reaching into the black Michael Kors cross bag that I was wearing, with no problem, I showed her my ID, and Mikel did the same.

"They're up on the 15th floor…you guys can go ahead and head up now. I've alerted them that you're on the way."

Quickly thanking her, we walked across the marble floors to the large gold elevators, and there was already one waiting on us.

"That security guard was everything," Mikel said, turning to me with a smirk on his face, holding his red Chanel bag on the side of him. My bestie almost never stepped out in sweats or not looking his best. He wore a red body-hugging tee with a pair of black skinny jeans and some red and black spiked Louboutin tennis shoes. To complete his fit, he wore a long black trench coat. This bitch was looking fire to say the least.

Me on the other hand, I was in my black sweats with my gray, white, and black Jordan 9s on. I didn't give a fuck though. Who was I tryna impress? Plus, my edges were laid, and my smooth chocolate skin was poppin' as always. I knew the weed had my already chinky eyes super low too, but fuck it…they were a security firm, not the police.

"Felicia?" a woman asked almost as soon as we walked off the elevator. The way their office was set up, once you were off the elevator, you were inside their space. The place was surrounded by windows with a bunch of desks and chairs spread about. Soft R&B music could be heard playing, and as I looked around, like a lightbulb coming on in my head, I noticed that the place was full of *only* women.

With my eyes as big as I could make them, I skeptically looked over at Mikel who was grinning, looking stupid as hell like he wanted to bust up laughing. Turning my attention back to the lady in front of us, I tried to calm my facial expression and at least see what they were talking about… maybe, this was just their office setting.

"I'm sorry about that. Yes, I'm Felicia. Are you Kateira?" I asked with my hand out, waiting for her to shake it.

"That's me. Let's go ahead and go to our conference room, so we can get down to business." Briefly shaking my hand, she wore a genuine smile against her even toned brown skin.

Once inside the conference room, the beautiful view overlooking the city of Oakland instantly took my breath away.

Already seated at the long rectangular-style table were two other women with extremely muscular builds. After Mikel and I took our seats, Kateira wasted no time getting started.

"So, for starters, I wanna go ahead and begin by introducing my two colleagues in the room. These are two of our top guards, and they come highly-recommended by our clients."

Standing up first was the taller of the two. Kateira introduced her as "Shanice," and if I had to guess...she had to be a little over six-feet tall. Wearing an all-black pants suit with a white silky-looking blouse underneath, to be honest, she looked like she could've been a detective or some shit. Even through her blazer, her muscular arms could easily be seen, and I also saw two.22s tucked behind her waist, letting me know that she wasn't someone to fuck with. The next woman was introduced as "Janae." She had doe-shaped bedroom eyes and wore her hair in a sleek ponytail pulled to the back. She was dressed almost identical to Shanice except her suit was blue, and she was packing two nine-millimeters.

After the introductions were done and everyone took their seats, once again, Kateira continued.

"Now that I've introduced the ladies, let me go ahead and tell you a little about our company. SATS was founded back in 2003. Our founder MaLia Anderson started our company after a rigorous search for employment within some of the top private security firms in the United States. She was turned away left and right after being told that this was a 'man's' business.

Resilient as ever, she didn't let that stop her. Teaming up with a few of her friends, they came together and built She's All That Security—the world's first all-female security firm—from the ground up. We are committed to providing only the highest level of service and proving to the world one person at a time that we can do this just as good as a man can."

After giving us a brief lesson on her company's history, Kateira definitely had me intrigued. The rest of the meeting was pretty much just us discussing numbers because, honestly, I was sold.

An all-black female security firm? We finna fuck some shit up, I thought to myself.

Without a second-thought, I signed a six-month contract with SATS and immediately chose Shanice and Janae. They were going to be starting as soon as we left the building.

After concluding the meeting and shaking Kateira's hand one final time, we all made our way to the elevators. Stopping before we got on, Katiera and the girls exchanged quick hugs before we went on our way.

As we rode the elevators back down to the lobby, it was awkwardly quiet as Mikel and I stole glances at each other before he childishly started snickering. Janae and Shanice were stone-faced with their hands resting together in front of them. They were not playing any games, and as the elevator doors opened, they made sure to be the first to step out. With their hands on their guns, they looked around quickly before they proceeded in front of us, like they were protecting the damn president or something.

"They finna hate our asses," Mikel whispered as he playfully nudged me, and we laughed together while walking behind the girls.

Once we made it back to my car, Kel went to open the driver's side door when Janae quickly stopped him, holding her hand out in front of him.

"Uhh, I apologize. We just usually handle the driving as well. Would that be okay?" she asked in a sweet voice when she saw the look on Mikel's face that said he was ready fight.

Rolling his eyes, he backed away with his hands up before opening the back door and climbing inside as I did the same. Glaring over at me, he reached up and opened the middle console before pulling a few blunts and lighter out. Sitting back down, he quickly lit up a blunt, placing the rest in the cupholder that divided us as Janae turned around with a smile.

"So, where we headed?" she asked as she briefly looked away to roll her window down.

"I think I'm going to head home, so I can change clothes and go into the office. It's been a while, and I got a bunch of work I need to catch up on. After you drop me off, you guys can take Kel wherever he needs to go and then wait for me back at the office. I'll text you when I'm on my way down, so feel free to go get food or whatever y'all need to do. My address is already preset in the GPS," I told her as she turned back around and started the GPS system without another word.

The whole way back to my house Mikel and I blew blunt after blunt before we departed for the day.

Once we made it, as I stepped out the back of the car, smoke flooded out into the air. It was Monday morning, and the sun shined brightly as we made our way into my house. After closing the door, I hurried to my room to change into something more appropriate for the office.

Pulling my sweatshirt over my head, I hurried to undress.

84

It was almost 10 a.m., and if I wanted to get any work done before the end of the day, I needed to get a move on. As I ran around like a tornado through my closet, I finally changed into a teal and white dress suit.

After accepting the blunt one final time, I decided on some open-toed strappy white heels that I'd had in my closet for years. Passing the blunt back to Mikel, I hurried to plug in my flat iron as I brushed my teeth again and sprayed on my favorite Calvin Klein perfume. Quickly running the flat iron over my hair, I was rocking it bone straight today. Looking at myself in the mirror, I applied a coat Nivea Chapstick to my full lips. Moving over to my closet, I grabbed my teal Birkin bag before heading for the door.

"Mikel, bring yo' ass on!" I yelled over my shoulder, realizing that he was still sitting on my bed.

"You need to shut up, bitch. I'm coming," he sneered as he eyed my outfit, "You ugly." Joking, he playfully bumped into me as he walked past.

"Thanks for letting me know I look cute, bitch."

Closing the door, I smiled to myself as I locked it.

"White girl voice activated," I said to myself as I hugged my best friend goodbye and exited the car.

*****

Walking inside the brightly lit office, all eyes were on me, and whispering voices filled with speculation were what greeted me. Keeping my head high with my laptop in hand, I went straight to my office and closed the door behind me.

The nerve of those motherfuckers! My fiancé gets killed, and everyone is looking at me like I'm on trial for murder. I don't know why I expected anything different.

85

It's not like they give a fuck. Even if they actually had offered their fake ass condolences, it would've held no value.

Logging onto my computer, I immediately got to work. I was behind on so much development that I didn't have time to dwell on the respect…or lack thereof, of my co-workers. I had a reputation to maintain, and even with the latest circumstances, I knew these companies wouldn't be too patient or understanding for much longer. I had three big projects that needed to be completed ASAP, and I didn't need any more distractions.

Grabbing my AirPods, I inserted them into my ears as I quickly turned on Pandora. With the music blasting, I was in my zone as I typed away effortlessly. I was designing customer relation software for an up-and-coming tech company, and the owner was very specific about what he wanted. Upon checking my emails, I saw that he was constantly asking for an update and reminding me of how things needed to be done.

I didn't need him up my ass any longer, so I decided to give 100% into getting this done as quickly as possible.

I was so wrapped up in the work that I was doing that, before I knew it, the sun had set. The usually chaotic office was now quiet. Leaning back in my chair, I finally looked away from my computer. Rubbing my eyes, I pulled my earbuds from out my ear and turned to look out at the night sky. As the thought of returning home crossed my mind, sadness engulfed me once again. I was missing Tristan so much that I'd give anything to feel him hold me again…hell, just to feel anyone hold me.

"Surprise!" I heard from behind me.

I slowly turned my chair around to face Rachel. She was standing there holding a big bouquet of red roses and a bottle of Bel-Air Rosé with the biggest grin on her face. I was so wrapped up in my own thoughts that I didn't even hear her come in.

Shaking off the mood I'd just climbed in, I quickly put on a smile as Rachel started walking towards me.

"I know you got my emails. I didn't wanna come in here on no depressing shit. I wanted to try to lift your spirits. I was about to leave but came up here and seen you deep in your work with no plans on going home anytime soon, so I'm staying with you. I got some glasses, and I can order whatever you want from UberEats…I know that I wouldn't want to be alone or at work right now, so I'm going to keep you company," she said, pulling out one of the chairs in front of my desk before taking a seat and pulling two champagne glasses from her purse. "…don't ask," she giggled after noticing the side-eye I was giving her as she pulled the wine glasses out.

I didn't feel like talking about Tristan's funeral or how I'd been feeling, and, luckily, she knew that. Time was going by so fast that we ended up spending and hour-and-a-half just talking and catching up on what I missed. Of course, Rachel had me cracking up with her impersonations of these uppity-ass white folks, and she even got me a little tipsy.

Standing up from behind my desk, I started packing up my laptop and gathering the notes that I'd been taking.

After packing my laptop bag with the work I still needed to finish, I rounded my desk before pulling Rachel in for a long hug. We never hung out outside of work, and, still, she knew exactly how my feelings were set up.

"Now, bitch, next time I invite you out, I don't wanna hear shit," she said as she tossed the empty bottle of wine into a recycling bin as we headed out of my office.

It was going on 9 o'clock, and the place was deserted. The only people here were the night janitors who made their rounds cleaning up the office under dim lighting.

Walking side by side, Rachel and I headed for the elevators as she recounted one of my employees who tried to step up in my absence.

"I'm telling you, Fe...you should've seen Mike's little-ass up here really thinking people was going to listen to him. Every time I came while you were gone, it was for pure comedy. Literally, the look on everyone's face anytime he spoke was just priceless," she chuckled, "I missed you so much, girl, and I know you hate sappy shit, but just know that if you ever need someone to talk to or just someone to keep you company, I'm only a call away."

"Ugh, I love yo' persistent-ass," I told her as I pulled her in for one more brief hug before we climbed inside the elevator.

Forgetting to text Shanice that I was on my way down, I was expecting them not to be here. However, once we made it down to the parking garage, there they were, eyes open and alert as ever.

After saying one last final goodbye to Rachel, I climbed into the back of the car as the ladies greeted me.

"Hey, Ms. Felicia, how was your day?" Shanice spoke up first.

"*Ugh,* tiring...I'm just ready to get home and climb straight in bed. I hope you guys weren't waiting on me too long," I said as I got comfortable in my seat and pulled a blunt from the cupholder beside me.

"No, we weren't waiting long, and even if we were, it's our job. We'll wait however long you need us too," Janae spoke genuinely as I lit the tip of my blunt.

Not saying another word, I took a pull from my blunt with my eyes closed as we rode under the night sky. As I smoked the loud trying to calm my nerves, my new second phone started ringing causing me to slowly open my eyes. Pulling the phone from my bag, I checked the screen and saw that it was Jacari. With no hesitation, I quickly answered, praying that he didn't have more bad news.

"Hello?"

"Hey, Fe, I know you said you was gon' handle things, but we found one of the locations where these niggas be trappin' at. They gettin' comfortable, and now's the time to let these niggas know what's really up. We finna send this nigga a wakeup call. I just wanted to run shit by you though. I can hit you up in the a.m. and let you know how everything went down," he spoke nonchalantly as I heard some other dudes in the back probably all getting hyped and ready to ride.

"Where y'all at right now?" I asked, sitting up in my seat as we neared my house.

"We at the basement right now, but we was 'bout to cut soon."

"Nah, y'all stay right there. I'm on my way. I'm not finna miss this opportunity to buss at these niggas. Wait for me," I told him before quickly ending the call.

Once we pulled inside my driveway, I asked the girls to wait for me as I quickly ran inside to switch out of this tight shit and put on some shit I could let loose in. With my all-black Air Force Ones and a black and dark-gray jogging suit on, I walked into my closet and grabbed my Glock.

After placing the gun inside my hoodie and grabbing my phone, I left everything else behind as I jogged back to the car.

"Janae, I need you guys to drop me off at the basement. It's also already preset in my GPS. You guys keep the car, and I'll call you in the morning when I'm ready for work," I told them as I sat back loading my gun.

"Are you sure, Ms. Felicia? It'd be no problem for us to wait," Shanice spoke.

"Just call me 'Felicia,' and I'm sure, you guys. Go home and get some rest," I told them as we entered the freeway.

Pulling up to the basement, I spotted a black Tahoe with Jacari and two other men leaned up against it smoking a blunt. As I exited the car, I heard one of them smack their lips, but I didn't pay it no mind as I approached them fearlessly. The night air was cool and chilling as we all stood outside with no words spoken.

"You sure about this, Fe? You ain't got shit to prove. We respect you just off GP, and even if you don't buss yo' gun, you still gon' be running this shit," Jacari said lowly as he walked closer to me.

"I'm sure, Cari. I don't need you worrying about me. I can handle myself…I promise. Now, let's go," I said as I jumped in the front seat of the car before placing my hand on my Glock and pulling it out of my pocket.

With the gun sitting on my lap and my hair pulled back into a tight ponytail, I sat straight up, staring blankly out the window as I felt Jacari's eyes on me.

"Huh, Fe, take the weed…you looking a lil' too tense over there."

"I'm good," I told him with a straight face as I turned to take the weed from his hand.

Chuckling to himself, he turned up the radio as he maneuvered the car and watched me at the same time. Webbie's old-school hit "G Shit" blared through the speakers as we rode, smoking multiple blunts at once.

After exiting off the freeway on Seminary, Cari turned the music down before he spoke.

"Y'all niggas have her back no matter what. I'll go in first, and y'all come in behind her. Stay on point. Tay, you especially 'cause I know how the weed gets you. Don't get caught slippin'," he said before turning the music back up.

Making a right-turn onto a tiny one-way street filled with old worn-down one-story houses, Jacari quickly cut the lights off and parked behind a bright red, beat-up, Honda. Reaching on the floor behind him, Cari pulled out a black pullover hoodie and a black trucker hat.

"You got ya' titties and shit showin', Fe. We ain't going jogging, and this shit ain't no game. Put these mothafuckas on, and let's go," he said coldly before reaching underneath his seat and pulling out a long barrel.22 rifle that glistened under the street lights as he loaded it.

Doing as I was told, I quickly pulled the hoodie over my head and placed the hat down low to my eyes as we jogged across the empty street.

Quietly moving up to the door of the old brown beat-up home, Jacari stood on the left side while I stood off in the shadows to the right. Tay and June were bent down low in front of the patio as we all waited for Cari to make the first move. My heart was beating so loudly that I thought maybe they could hear it too before I realized it was just in my head. As many times as I'd shot a gun before, I've never actually fired one off at somebody...well, besides Bleek.

As hard as I was trying to act inside, I was nervous as hell. My palms were sweating, and I was constantly rubbing them off on my pants as I finally heard Jacari knock. Wiping my hands one final time, I took a deep breath before a tall, lanky, ugly-ass, black dude pulled the door open with a scowl on his face.

Moving quickly, Cari used the butt of his gun, knocking the fool back inside the house. Following his lead, we all entered the room after him with our guns drawn, ready to murk anything moving. With blood rapidly leaking from his mouth and nose, the dude confusingly looked up at us before he spoke.

"Fuck ya'll niggas want?" he asked before spitting blood on the floor right in front of Jacari's boot.

"You know what this is, nigga...where's the money and the yayo?" Cari asked while moving his gun.

"You must think I was bitch-made."

Rolling my eyes, I was already tired of hearing his voice. Moving quickly and without thought, I stepped forward, firing off a single shot into his arm.

Pop!

"Next one going in ya' skull. Stop playing, nigga."

"*Ahhhh!*" he screamed out in agony as blood started seeping from the hole in his arm.

"It's upstairs, man...shit!" he hollered as he tried to cover the wound with his hand to stop the bleeding.

Grabbing him by the arm I'd just shot him in, Jacari roughly pulled him off the floor as we all went up the stairs. June and Tay stayed behind.

With my gun aimed at the back of this bitch-nigga's head, all my nervousness had vanished. The thought of him being involved or even running with the nigga who killed Tristan fueled me. I was itching to put one in the back of his head, but I'd be damned if we didn't find the money and work first.

Reaching the top of the stairs, I stood back on the top step as the nigga pointed us in the direction of a closed door.

"Open the mothafucka up," Cari instructed as he pushed the dude so hard that he tripped.

Getting up off the floor with a cold mug on his face, he turned the nob and pushed the door open. With a single dim light on, it appeared to be empty. With the shotty aimed on the leaking D-boy, Jacari cautiously continued on before allowing him entrance first.

Once he made it inside, some nigga thought it was cool to jump out like a jack-in-the-box.

Pop!

Letting off a shot of his own, the clown dropped Jacari to the floor. My heart was beating so fast inside my chest before my instincts kicked in. Watching him kick Jacari's gun to the side, the nigga obviously didn't even know I was there too.

"Who you work for, brah?" he asked, giving Jacari all of his attention.

Moving closer to the door, I replied, "Me" before I let my Glock whistle, sending five shots into his chest, dropping him instantly to his knees.

I watched as blood escaped from his wounds with only one thing on my mind—Tristan. All this was for him.

Turning my attention back to the other pussy in the room who was sitting on the floor quiet as a mouse still nursing his wound, after what just went down and hearing my voice, he now looked scared shitless. Giving him a look that said don't fuck with me, I bent down to check on Jacari. Luckily, he was only hit in his shoulder blade and was still breathing. He must've just passed out from the impact.

Looking around the room, I didn't see any water, so I did the first thing that came to my mind.

Whap!

I slapped Jacari as hard as I could because I needed him to get up.

Quickly jumping up off the floor, his eyes were big as hell as he stood with his fists up.

"'Bout time you re-joined us," I laughed as I got up off the floor with my gun in hand.

"Fe, I know you didn't just fucking slap me, brah?" With blood still trickling down his arm from his wound, Jacari was furious.

June and Tay came walking up the stairs with confused looks on their faces, I'm sure trying to piece together what happened in their minds.

"I have no idea what you're talking 'bout, Cari. Pick ya' gun up and focus back on the poodle in the corner please," I said, trying not to smile too hard.

Turning our attention to the young nigga, June hurried to snatch him off the floor as Jacari retrieved his shotgun. Carrying him over to the safe, the nigga wasted no time as he quickly put the combination in.

"That's everything, y'all...I swear. Please, don't kill me. I got a baby on the way," he pleaded as tears welled up in his eyes.

"You one of these niggas who's been running 'round here talking 'bout y'all took out the hottest nigga in the Bay, ain't you?" I asked looking him dead in his eyes.

"Nah, I don't know what you talking about, man. Please, just let me go."

His loyalty was truly heartwarming, but that shit wasn't gonna get him no badge of honor fuckin' with me. Heartlessly, I pulled my gun up before letting off a single shot splattering his brains onto the wall. Without saying anything, they all were looking at me like I had lost my mind before hurrying to empty the safe.

The whole ride back to the basement was a silent one.

CHAPTER ELEVEN

I woke up the next morning with tears streaming down my face from the dream I had. Tristan was lying in bed with me, and it all felt so real. I was lying on his chest while he stroked my hair gently and told me that everything was going to be okay. The most vivid part of the dream though was him telling me not to let this game turn me cold and to stay true to myself.

Sitting up, I wiped my wet face before I went to get started on my hygiene. As I looked back at my reflection in the mirror, I felt dead inside. With Tristan gone, a big piece of me had died too, and, in a way, I almost didn't recognize myself. I had murdered two men yesterday, and the thought of how their families were grieving or if they left behind any kids didn't even cross my mind. All I could think about was the pain that I was still feeling and the children *I* would never get to have.

Picking up my phone, I sent my security a quick text letting them know that I'd be ready in about thirty-minutes before I quickly hopped in the shower. Once I finished, in just my bra and panties, I applied a little concealer to the huge bags that started to form underneath my eyes.

After deciding on a navy-blue skirt, white blouse, and these vintage navy, gray, and white Chanel heels and matching bag, I was ready to go.

As I climbed into the back seat of my car, my phone started ringing from inside my purse. It was Mikel.

"Good morning, *biiiitchh!*" he shouted as soon as I answered.

"Good morning, bestie."

Closing the car door, I got situated before putting him on speaker phone.

"Hey, ladies, good morning. We're headed to the office." Greeting my security, I grabbed a blunt from my middle console and fired up.

"Hoe, are you dumb? Do you *not* hear me talking to you?" Mikel's screaming had me about to choke on smoke with his extra-ass.

"Ugh, you get on my damn nerves," I laughed, "I'm sorry, best friend. I'm all ears."

"Let's go out tonight! I keep on hearing about this new lounge called the Money Room. They just opened up in Downtown Oakland. We haven't been out in so long, bitch...I'm not taking 'no' for an answer."

Looking out at the water as we neared the Bay Bridge, I contemplated hard on if I was down for Mikel's antics on this good Friday. When we did used to go out clubbing every other weekend, it was always some drama, somebody bumping Mikel too hard or tryna get slick.

Rolling my eyes, I listened as he tried to convince me that there wouldn't be no bullshit this time.

"Best friend, I promise you...no drama, no fighting, nothing. Just dancing and popping pussy, V.I.P., big bottles, all that. Come on, bitch, you know how we do it." I could tell he was grinning as he spoke. He was obviously geeked and really wanted to do this, so being the ride or die I am, although I didn't want to, I agreed.

"A'ight, nigga, meet me at my house later. I'll call you when I'm on my way home," I told him through gritted teeth as I rolled my eyes. His ass better be lucky I loved him.

"Don't sound so dry, bitch! We're gonna have fun. Love you, BF."

"I love you too, ugly."

Ending the call, I looked out at the water as we approached the toll bridge to enter San Francisco. With everything going on around me, the last thing I needed to do was to be partying, but it was also the exact reason why I agreed. I needed to feel normal again. It was beginning to feel like I was getting lost in finding revenge for Tristan, so, tonight, I wanted to forget about everything. I just wanted good vibes, music, and love around me.

Finally pulling into the parking garage of my office building, I said my goodbyes to the ladies before heading upstairs. It was already 9:30 a.m., and I wanted to get an early start today.

As I rode the elevator up, I checked my reflection in my phone before putting my game face on. These white men where ruthless. Any signs of weakness shown, and I knew they'd be coming for my job like a pack of hungry wolves.

Stepping off the elevator, I was greeted with the smell of fresh coffee and donuts. As I walked past, I noticed a few people gathered in our kitchen area laughing and talking until I walked by. Laughing to myself, I just continued to my office before closing the door behind me. The deadline for the CRM software I'd been working on was today, and I planned to crank out these last little bugs fast as hell with *no* interruptions.

Inserting my AirPods, I turned on my soft jazz and R&B playlist before pulling out my laptop and escaping the world. Whenever I was working, it felt like nothing else mattered. I put everything into my work; this was my passion. Developing new technological ways for companies to monitor and better interact with their consumers was truly only the beginning to what I could do. This was going to be a breeze.

As I tirelessly worked on completing my project, the last person I expected to see knocked on my door. It was the CEO of my company Brian McKinney. He stood outside my door wearing an impatient expression on his handsome face.

"I'm sorry to keep you waiting, sir. I was so focused on finishing up the JDX project. Please, excuse my manners," I told him as I rushed to open the door.

"Thanks, Felicia. How has your day been so far?" he asked before getting situated in one of the plush chairs in front of my desk.

"*Ehh,* I can't complain, sir. I'm breathing. How are you though? And how are Kirsten and Analiyah?"

Taking a seat back in my chair, I turned to face him with a solemn expression.

"They're good. Analiyah just made 3 last month, and, man, I can't even tell you how amazing it is just watching her grow. The other day she told Kirsten that she wanted to go for manicures. Manicures, Felicia! Can you believe that?"

Pulling out his phone, he briefly showed me a few pictures of his beautiful little girl. She truly was growing up fast. I remembered when he returned to the office from his leave after she was first born. He had so much pride as he shared her pictures with me.

Whenever he was actually in the office or had free-time, he always made sure he came to see how I was doing mentally and just to catch up. Our little conversations actually meant so much to me, and I was grateful for his impartiality. He didn't see skin color or even gender when he picked me for this role. He measured my work ethic, passion, and saw my resilience when it came to any project or task I was given. It was just truly an honor for him to be my predecessor.

"Oh, my god! Look at her…those nail colors are everything and her little purse! I just can't deal. She is so beautiful, sir."

Handing him his phone back, he looked at me with concern in his eyes.

"Are you sure you're really okay? You know if you need more time off or just need to talk, I'm here. I didn't know Tristan well, but I know this can't be easy for you." Getting serious, he sat up in his chair and looked me straight in the eyes as he spoke.

"No, sir, I'm good. My work makes me feel…I don't know if you'll understand, but it makes me feel like I'm at home. It's when I'm most in my comfort zone, so, if anything, being here is helping me more than you could even know," I told him honestly.

Getting up from his seat, he smiled at me as I took in his appearance. He was standing at maybe 6'2, wearing an expensive unknown designer suit that was tailored to fit him perfectly. His low cut curly hair and full neatly trimmed beard was on point as it always. He was looking good as fuck, but I kept my thoughts in my head as I focused back on him standing before me.

"Come on, bring it in," he said as he rounded my desk and pulled me up for a friendly side hug, "Really, don't work too fucking hard. You got nothing to prove to these assholes. If you need any…"

"I know, sir…just give you a call."

"Hell, text, email…however you want to get in touch with me, I'm here. Oh, and we've talked about the 'sir' thing too many times, Felicia. 'Brian' will be fine," he said with finality while laughing to himself on the way out the door.

Focusing back on the work in front of me, I started putting the final touches on the software. I worked past lunch and well into the day unconsciously. When I finally finished working and testing everything out, it was already 5:30 p.m. Getting up from behind my desk, I decided to take a breather. Walking from out of my office for the first time today, I went to invade our fully stocked kitchen. We kept all kinds of snacks and drinks available for anyone who worked here.

As I rounded the corner into the kitchen, the conversation between the two men sitting at a small table ceased. Moving around the room, I grabbed a Bai kiwi-flavored water from the fridge before grabbing Hot Cheetos, fruit snacks, and cashews from the cabinets. All the while I could feel the uneasiness they felt just off of my presence alone, and I loved it. White people have had that effect on us for way too long.

That was also another reason why I loved my job. I knew that I made these men uncomfortable and kept them on their toes. It was such an invigorating feeling that was really almost unexplainable.

With my snacks and drink, I headed back to my office smirking as I heard them immediately start back talking.

Just as I was about to close my door, I noticed Rachel walking up from the corner of my eye. She wasn't looking like her usual happy self, so I knew something had to be wrong. Proceeding into my office, I sat down and opened the Hot Cheetos while waiting for her to come inside.

"Oh, shit, close the door," I told her as soon as she entered looking as if she was about to cry. "What's going on, Rach?" I asked while snacking on my chips.

"Ugh, girl, it's nothing. I'm just going through it with my man. I'll be all right. I came up here to check on you though. How are you today, chica?"

Putting on the fakest smile, I looked back at her confusingly.

"I didn't even know you had a man. I be talking your ear off all day long about Tristan, but you haven't told me about this man of yours. Oh, hell no, bitch…spill the tea."

As I opened my fruit snacks, I waited for her to give me the details.

"I haven't talked about him because it's still new, but he's driving me crazy already. He's so possessive and controlling. The shit has just been stressing me out. I need a damn drink forreal." I knew that she was hinting yet again at us going out after work, so I thought what the hell?

"Me and my bestie are going out to this new lounge called the Money Room in Oakland tonight. You should come with us. It sounds like you could use some fun just as much as I do," I told her as I threw all of my wrappers into the trash.

"*Yasss,* bitch, finally! You know I'm down. Just text me the address, and I'll meet y'all up there. Now, I gotta rush home and find something to wear. I'm so excited though. I guess I'll just see you up there!"

In a way better mood than she was in when she came in, Rachel got up and hurried out of my office.

Now ready to go, I began packing up my things before sending a text to my security letting them know I was on my way downstairs. Tonight was going to be interesting. Honestly, my flaky-ass felt like backing out already, but what could a few drinks hurt?

Trying to be optimistic about the night, I rode the elevator thinking tonight was going to be a good night. I was hoping true to people's words that the power of my thoughts would really come through. The last thing I needed in my life right now was *more* bullshit.

*****

Once, I made it home, Mikel was already parked out in front of my house waiting on me to pull up.

"Damn, tramp, took you long enough. Let's go, let's go! We gotta pull yo' ass together pronto!"

The whole way up my driveway, he was just rambling on about how lit it was finna be and how we'd been needing this.

Trying to keep my thoughts to myself, I acted like I was juiced too and hurried to unlock my door. The first thing he did once we were inside was go straight into my freezer and grab a bottle of Cîroc that he knew I kept faithfully stocked inside. With two mini-red cups and the bottle in hand, he barged into my room full of excitement.

"*Owwweee,* it's finna be lit, bitch…perk up!" he told me before pouring two shots and handing one to me first.

Taking the small cup from his hand, without hesitation, I threw the shot back and handed the empty cup over to him. I wasn't sure about tonight, but I knew that after a few more shots, I wouldn't even give a fuck anymore.

Turning on my Beats Pill, Mikel connected his phone before Drake's "Nice for What" started pounding throughout the room.

"That's a real one in your reflection without a follow, without a mention. You really pippin' up on these niggas. You gotta be nice for what to the niggas?"

As the music played, we moved around the room like a hurricane, trying on different outfits and shoes. Kel was adamant about finding me the perfect fit.

Once it was all said and done, I looked at my reflection in the mirror, and tears came to my eyes. Flashbacks of Tristan walking up behind me while I wore this same outfit hit me like a strike of lightning. It was like I could really feel his touch around my waist, but I knew that it couldn't be.

Zoning out in the mirror, I stood there as tears silently fell before Mikel danced his silly-ass over to me. Two-stepping and smiling, he came over and grabbed my hand motioning for me to dance with him.

"Come on, bitch, just like *Grey's Anatomy,* we finna dance it out. I'm not finna let this shit drive you crazy. I know you love him, Fe, but you have to know that you will live on without him. Now, dance, bitch!" Gently shoving me, he grinned before jumping around looking like a damn fool, just like Meredith and Christina had in the show, reminding me why he was my person…my one I'd call to help me bury a body, and no questions would be asked.

Joining him, I started jumping from side-to-side really offbeat with not a care in the world as tears continued to fall from my face. We danced into they turned to laughter at each other's crazy dance moves before I pulled my best friend in for a hug. The road ahead was not going to be an easy one, but I liked knowing that no matter what, I would have Mikel with me.

CHAPTER TWELVE

As we exited the back of my car with my security looking like they would bust at anything that got too close, all eyes were on us. It seemed to be a really chill setting though. I didn't hear any extra loud music or see the usual ratchets. Everyone was stressed down in their finest and looking good. There were a few bitches who needed some help with their heads, but that was none of my business though.

Chuckling to myself, Mikel and I walked straight to the front of the line and were immediately allowed entrance into the lounge.

"Felicia! Felicia!" I heard someone shout from behind me, and when I turned around, I saw Rachel getting held back by security. Kel was looking so confused, like *who is this dumb broad?* as I walked over to let them know that she was with us.

Walking back with my arm linked into Rachel's, I saw the look on Mikel's face that said he was ready to start some shit. Moving over to his side, I introduced them before he got petty.

"Rachel, this is my best friend Mikel. Kel, this is Rachel...the one I always tell you about from work," I said, slightly nudging him so that he'd get the hint to fix his face.

"You ain't tell me you invited nobody else, bitch. Why is Miss Empanada here?" He was trying to whisper, but I was almost sure that Rachel had heard him.

"Excuse me…why is *who* here?" she spoke up and started an all-out bickering match that I didn't have the time for. I didn't come here for this stupid shit.

Walking off from them without either of them even noticing, I walked to the bar and was finally able to take in the ambiance. There were beige-colored walls with small seating areas that had white intimate loveseats carefully placed about. The bar was a long slab of beautiful marble that had a bunch of matching marble shelves along the wall behind it. Lit tea candles were flickering on each row. Underneath the bottles of alcohol, a soft blue light illuminated the names of the drinks. The whole setting was just such a vibe.

Placed in front of the bar were a bunch of unique white rectangular stools that were already taken. As light hip hop music played, everyone was mingling and appeared to be having good conversations. Squeezing in between someone who I paid no mind to, I waved my hand to get the bartender's attention.

"Two shots of Crown Royal Black please?" I asked once he made his way over to me.

Standing at the bar wearing an all-black long sleeve pants jumpsuit that tied at the waist and clung to my body paired with some YSL strappy heels, I knew I was looking good. They were the Tower Stiletto edition and were embellished with crystals around the ankle strap and heel. I couldn't remember when I bought them, but I knew that they had the attention of a lot of women in the room.

As the bartender returned with my shots, one after the other, I quickly downed them both before turning around to find Mikel and Rachel's crazy asses. I wasn't really a drinker and knew that soon enough I'd be joining them in their foolishness if I didn't slow down. I just couldn't shake the feeling that I didn't belong here and that I should've been at home mourning the loss of my fiancé.

Trying to keep my mind on anything but Tristan, I strutted away from the bar. I didn't know what the hell Mikel had been hearing, but somebody lied…this place was dry as hell.

Spotting him and Rachel seated on one of the loveseats calmly talking, I walked over to them now happy that they were getting along.

As I maneuvered through people to get to my friends, a man blocked my path with a cocky smile on his face. Before me stood a fine-ass chocolate hunk who resembled Morris Chestnut. He had a strong jawline that he clenched before he spoke and soft bedroom eyes that were staring into mine attentively. His full pink lips were moving, but I couldn't hear a word as my body started to heat up, and, instantly, I felt ashamed. It wasn't like I fucked him, but it was way too soon to even be thinking about another man.

Focusing back on his eyes, he smiled a slight beautiful smile and flexed his pearly whites before I found my voice.

"I apologize…what did you say?" I asked him in almost a whisper. My voice was still caught in my throat because this man had my body on fire. My pussy was dripping just from the sight of him like a dog in heat or something.

Doing my best to focus, I heard him say, "My name is Seth. How are you doing tonight?" He spoke in a monotone voice, deep and consistent.

"I'm Felicia…and I'm doing all right. Thank you for asking." Chuckling for no reason at all, it felt like all the shots I'd taken finally started to hit me.

"So, uh, can I get you a drink? If you'd like, you can join me in my section, so we can continue our conversation. I'd really like to get to know you a little better, Ms. Felicia." Coming closer to my ear with the last words that he spoke, I'm sure he felt the effect that he was having on my body as he reached around and pulled me close to him, causing me to damn-near climax just off his touch. I had to get away from him.

Pushing him back, I hurried over to my friends without saying another word, hoping that he wouldn't approach me again.

"Okay, bitch, who was that?" Mikel grilled as soon as I was within earshot.

"I don't fucking know, but he's doing something to me. Tell me he's not walking over here."

Nervously standing in front of them on the loveseat, I knew my answer by the looks on their faces and the scent of expensive cologne in the air. He was definitely coming over here, and he was close.

"I apologize if I was too aggressive, but, damn, look how beautiful you are. Again, I apologize if I was being too forward. I hope you don't feel disrespected because that was the last thing I was trying to do. I really just want to get to know you better if you'll allow me to."

Walking up behind me, he started speaking without me even turning around to face him.

Rolling my eyes, I childishly replied, "Sorry, I'm not interested."

Closing my eyes, I hoped and prayed that he'd just go away. The sensations he was giving me were ones only my fiancé could, and for them to be coming from a stranger made me feel dirty.

"He's gone now, Fe," I heard Kel say closer than he was before. When I opened my eyes, he was standing

109

right in front of me looking like a concerned parent. He and Rachel both looked worried before he brought his hand up and wiped my cheek. I hadn't even realized that tears were forming in my eyes until one actually fell.

"I'm good, you guys. The drank must've had me tripping for a sec. Stop worrying about me and go mingle…have some fun," I told them, forcing myself to muster up the most genuine smile I could.

Rachel was obviously satisfied with my response as she turned to go get a drink, but Mikel knew better.

"Uhn uhh, bitch, you tried it. Let's go. You may be able to fool Miss Jenny from the block, but you ain't foolin' me. I'm sorry I pushed you to do this shit earlier than you were ready to. Let's just go. We can do this shit at home anyway. This club is dry as shit." Playfully rolling his eyes, we both broke out in laughter.

Linking his arm within mine, my bestie tilted his head against my shoulder as we searched for Rachel preparing to leave. What's understood didn't need to be spoken, so we didn't waste time talking about my feelings. We just agreed that it was time to go.

"We finna bonk out Rochelle" Kel joked as we approached Rachel.

"Fe, I thought you *just* said you were cool…what the hell?" Taking a sip of her drink, she truly just didn't get it.

"We know what she said, and she is fine, but we're leaving. Now, ju can either come with us, mami, or ju can stay. I don't give a damn either way," Mikel told her being childish, mimicking a Spanish-accent. This was why I didn't take his ass nowhere.

"Mikel, you know you need to quit," I said as I cut my eyes at him even though I wanted to bust out laughing, "Rach, I'm sorry, but I'm just not feeling it, boo. We'll have plenty more chances to do this, so don't be mad at me." Poking out my bottom lip, I waited to know that she was cool.

"Yeah whatever, hoe, long as you don't flake like you usually do, but I understand. My man was gon' slide through anyway, so I'll be fine. I'll call you later to check on you and make sure you're good. Love you, girl." Bringing me in for a hug, we said our goodbyes before Mikel and I finally headed towards the exit.

On our way out, the same guy from before pulled my hand to get my attention.

"Excuse me, miss, I hope I'm getting it right this time. I mean no disrespect, but your beauty just won't let me let you walk out that door without a proper introduction. My name is Seth Bivens. I'm just here with a few of my friends, not looking to cause any trouble," he said, smiling as he revealed those perfect white sparkly white teeth and beautiful smile that made my heart skip a beat. Once again, I was frozen in place before Kel spoke up.

"She's coo, brah," he told him, grabbing my arm and pulling me towards the exit but not before the handsome stranger jogged over and handed me his card.

CHAPTER THIRTEEN

Three-months later…

After the night we hit one Josiah's traps, everything had been smooth sailings. I felt like it was weird that he and his boys just fell back, but they didn't even know who they were coming after in the first place.

It had been three-months, and there hadn't been any drama. Everything was running smoothly, and I even re-upped from Emiliano twice already. I'm sure with Tristan's death, everyone was wondering who had taken over, but no one had yet to figure out that it was me. Money was pretty much falling in at this point, and, truth be told, I was running out of places to put it.

After weeks of debating, I finally decided to move. I found a nice little house not too far from here, and, today, I was moving in.

Packing up my place brought back so many memories of Tristan. I couldn't help but feel emotional. In a way, it felt like I was leaving him here, and that made it so hard for me to actually leave. For the sake of my sanity though, I had to get out of here. The happy memories that Tristan and I once shared had quickly faded and were replaced with ones of tears and sadness.

Walking into his closet and smelling the scent of his cologne or seeing his clothes caused me to almost have a stroke each time. I was looking forward to finally being able to have my peace of mind back, but I didn't wanna completely erase Tristan's memory either.

Stepping into his side of our closet, I ran my fingers along the fabric of his clothes that were hanging neatly and unused. Looking ahead of me, I stood in awe as I looked up at his boxes of shoes stacked all the way up to the ceiling. They were all placed on a remote-controlled carousel that would move up and down as needed. There were Jordans, Louboutins, Balenciagas, and so many other designers that I didn't even feel like looking through them all.

As much as I knew these things would be appreciated by someone else in need, I just couldn't bring myself to donate them. I'd lose my damn mind if I was rolling down the street and saw some random dude wearing his favorite Balmain jacket. The fact of the matter was that these clothes were all I had left of him, and they weren't going anywhere.

After taking a deep breath, I slowly started removing his things from the hangers. Neatly folding his clothes, I placed them inside a huge box that I planned to put into a storage unit. As I continued folding and placing more things inside the box, my doorbell rang. The blunt I smoked earlier obviously had me a little paranoid because I jumped at the sound. Mikel would never ring my doorbell, and I wasn't expecting anybody else.

Grabbing my nine, I slowly walked into my living room area before quietly moving towards the door. Wearing just some pajama shorts and an old white t-shirt that I'd had for years, I peeked into the peephole before exhaling quickly in confusion. It was my little brother Adam. I hadn't spoken to him or any of my brothers since Tristan passed, so questions of what the fuck he was doing here ran rapidly through my mind.

113

Running over to my couch, I quickly tucked the gun underneath one of the base pillows.

"Open the door, Fe. I know ya' ass in there. I see all these cars out here," he yelled as he rang the bell once again.

With my back against the door, I rolled my eyes up into my head before I unlocked it and swung it open.

"What the fuck are you doing here, Adam? You don't own a phone?" I asked, still standing in my doorway, not wanting to let him in. I didn't need him fishing for information just to take it back to my other brothers and start some bullshit.

"Damn, sis, it's like that? You was heavy on my mind, so I thought I'd surprise you. You really not finna let me in?" he asked, now with a serious look on his goofy face.

Adam was the youngest of my brothers and the baby of the family. He was spoiled as hell and didn't really experience the struggle like the rest of us had. With my dad not being in our lives, my mom always tried to make up for his absence with material things for Adam. At 18, he never had a job but owned a car, stayed in the latest designer shit, and always had the latest iPhone. He had smooth peanut butter skin like my mother, and his brown almond-shaped eyes were adorned with long beautiful lashes. He kept a clean fade and had just gotten his braces taken off, so his coke white smile only added to his swagger.

Standing before me in some acid washed Robin's jeans that were sagging way too low, red and white Jordan 11s, and a red Chicago Bulls jacket with a plain white tee underneath, his ugly-ass thought he was cute.

Stepping back from the door, I finally allowed him into my house and grilled his ass as he walked past me.

"So, wassup, sis? What you been up to? You don't know how to call your brothas no more or what?" he asked as he took a seat on my couch and pulled out a bag of weed and swishers to roll a blunt.

"I've had a lot going on, Adam. And, a phone works both ways; y'all niggas ain't think to call me." Rolling my eyes in my head, I grabbed another empty box and started wrapping my vases with newspaper.

"Yeah, I can see that you've fa sho had a whole bunch of shit going on," he said, reaching under my couch pillow and pulling out my nine.

"I knew this mothafucka felt a lil' lumpy, but, damn, sis, who needs this type of protection, and where's Tristan?" he asked in a funny tone that made me think he already knew.

"…he was murdered a few months ago." Hanging my head, I felt slightly ashamed that I hadn't called my family.

"You don't fucking say. We've all been knew, but the fact that you didn't call yo' family or feel like you couldn't lean on us, yo' brothers especially, had us all fucked up. So, we decided to give you yo' space, but my nigga called me and told me that he'd been hearing about a female taking over Tristan's territory." Pausing to lick the swisher closed, he looked at me to check my reaction, but I just kept on packing. "So, I figured, I needed to pay my big sis a visit," he continued before sparking his blunt, "I just gotta know for myself…you ain't out here being reckless, is you? You fucking with the dope game, Fe, fareal?" His eyebrows were raised as he inhaled smoke from his blunt before blowing a thick cloud in my direction.

"Hell nah…I don't know why these niggas be talking like bitches. I have a job, Adam. I don't have time for no

115

bullshit." Smacking my lips, I never made eye contact with him as I continued moving around my living room wrapping and placing things where they belonged.

"So, who took over Tristan's business then? And, why you ain't hit us up about that shit, Fe? I know you had a say in whoever it went to," he assumed.

"Tristan's boys handled all that shit. I had way too much on my plate to even care where it went," I told him as I finally came and took a seat next to him. "Enough with the questions like this is an interrogation or some shit though…let me hit the weed," I said before snatching the bag of tree he had.

Ever since he first started smoking, anytime he had weed, I always took some just on the principle that he wasn't supposed to have it.

"Come on, man, chill. You always doing that shit."

As he tried to snatch the bag back from me, I realized how much I'd missed him. His voice had grown deeper, and he was constantly getting taller.

"So, nigga, while you all up in my business, how's school?" I asked, getting serious before handing him back the bag as he inspected how much I took.

"Shit, school is school. I'm glad I chose an HBCU though because this experience has just been crazy. I'm learning so much about our history and meeting so many dope souls," he said with his eyes low, cheesing hard as hell. My baby brother attended Charles Drew University of Medicine and Science. He was majoring in computer engineering under the influence of his big sister, so to say I was proud was an understatement.

Like me, he didn't let the weed cloud his mind but used it to balance out the lows that life often handed out.

As we sat and caught up with each other, smoking blunts and watching TV, I felt more at home here than I had in a while. I didn't realize how important the love and support of my brothers were.

"Sis, I didn't only come down here 'cause I missed you. Truthfully, if I tell you some shit, you gotta promise to keep it between me and you."

"Nigga, when have you known me to run my mouth? Spill it! I'm listening," I said, giving him my undivided attention.

"Well, I was looking for a way to stand on my own two feet. I mean, I know you, Mom, and everybody always look out for me, and I never want for shit, but I've been feeling like I need to be my own man," he spoke honestly, and for the first time, I stopped seeing him as my little nerdy-ass brother and started seeing him as the young man he was. Not wanting to interrupt, I just let him continue. "So, my boy Bernard had this lil' plug he put me on to, and what I thought was gon' be just a side hustle has actually become really profitable."

"Wait a minute, you talking about weed? You been profiting off weed?"

"I mean, you say that like it ain't possible...but, nah, Fe. I've been fucking with that white girl," he told me as he grinned, looking high as hell.

In an instant, my smile had faded as I walked over and slapped him hard as fuck upside the back of his head.

"You're doing what now, dumbass?" I asked as he grabbed the back of his head, looking up at me through confusion-filled blood red eyes.

"I've been making my own fucking money if you didn't already hear me," he said as he nonchalantly shrugged his shoulders and looked me dead in my eyes.

"Adam, are you dumb, nigga? Do you know what you're risking? Your future and your career so that you can feel like a *man?* You could've went and got a real

117

job like the rest of the world, dummy! I know for a fact you not that stupid. You got me ready to slap the shit out of you right now," I told him as I walked into my kitchen. I needed to put space between us before I got my belt and whooped his ass like he was my own child. I was livid. All of the opportunities and everything he had going for himself, and this was what he decided to do.

"If I knew you were gonna blow up like this, I wouldn't've said shit," I heard him mumble, and I started to feel a little bad. I didn't want to ruin the bond we had, but I also didn't want him to think that I was cool with what he was doing either.

"I didn't mean to spaz on you, but what the fuck? How'd you expect me to react? Tristan lost his life for doing some of the same shit you are. No matter how small you dealin' or how smart you think you moving, anything can happen, Adam. I love you, so I'ma keep it real with you…the shit is dumb. If you needed help getting a job, you could've asked. I mean, anything but this shit."

"Ain't nobody looking for me or none of the crazy shit you thinking, Fe. It's good. I came out here to see if you could put me in touch with some of Tristan's boys 'cause I need a new connect but judging from your reaction…I see that ain't gon' happen, so I'ma just go back to campus. I love you, sis."

Preparing to leave, he got up and tried to come and hug me goodbye, but I held my hand up, stopping him.

"I'm not finna help you with that, but you ain't gotta leave. I'm moving today, and I could use the extra help." I was hoping he'd agree to stay, so that I could talk some sense into him.

*****

Mikel, Jacari, Adam, and I were all tired as hell after moving all my things into my new place. They all complained the whole time, saying that I should've hired movers, but fuck that. I wasn't trusting nobody with all my shit.

As we sat around with only my couches set up, eating pizza, and talking shit, my baby brother fit right in. Jacari had become my right-hand man, handling all the distro and collecting all the dough when I couldn't. He had become a close friend and helped guide me in this unknown world I had entered.

"Ay, Fe, I saw ya' girl and Josiah out at dinner yesterday. They was at Ruth's Chris all boo'd up in a little candlelit booth. I mean, I ain't no psychic, but the bitch looking like she getting real comfortable…was staring at the nigga all googly-eyed. Have they checked in with you recently?" Jacari asked before passing me a blunt that was already lit.

With so much going on, I damn-near forgot that I had the twins working on that nigga. They went and met him at one of his clubs a while back, but after everything jumped off at one Josiah's traps, I told them to fall back.

As I inhaled the weed, my thoughts were running a mile per minute as I thought about why they'd still be dealing with that nigga.

Passing the blunt to Adam, I walked to the back of the house and pulled my cellphone from the pocket of my shorts. Wearing only a tank top and some of Tristan's basketball shorts, I dialed Nalia, hoping that I could get some answers. It was going on 10:30 p.m. I wasn't sure if she'd answer, but I had to know what was going on.

"Hello?" she answered just as I assumed her voicemail was about to come on.

"Hey, girl, this Felicia. What y'all hoes up to?" I asked as leaned against my window frame with the phone to my ear.

"Oh, hey, Fe...I wasn't doing shit, just in bed watching TV. What you up to, girl?"

"The same, bored as hell. Where's Talia's ass at? I'm surprised y'all not out chasing a bag."

"Girl, she with some new nigga she been fuckin' with. He's been keeping my sissy away from me, taking her on all these trips and shit, but that's cool though. I'ma find me a man," she said, sounding bitter as hell.

"The right one will come along for you. Don't even trip, girl," I told her honestly.

"Yeah, and it will happen again for you too. Keep yo' head up, Fe," she said genuinely.

"Thanks, girl. I was just calling to check in with you guys though. It's been a minute."

"Yeah, we've been cool, Fe. Since you canceled that job, we've just been chillin'."

"A'ight, well, y'all already know if you need anything, just hit me up," I told her before ending the call.

Standing in my new empty room, my mind was all over the place. If Talia decided to still fuck with Josiah, I needed to know why. Luckily, I didn't give them any real information about my business, but that shit just wasn't sitting right with me. When the time came for me to put a bullet into Josiah's skull, Talia just better hope that she wasn't around. Old friends or not, I wouldn't hesitate to leave her ass stankin' too.

Walking in the room behind me, my little brother sported a serious expression. He carried a presentation folder with him that he held out for me to take. Looking up at him confused, he gave me a confident smile in return.

"Just read through it, Fe," he said as I walked into the master bathroom to turn on the light. Leaning up against the marble countertop, I flipped through the pages, and with each page, I became more and more intrigued. Adam and his friend had created a startup delivery service. On paper, they appeared to be like any other service like DoorDash or UberEats. Judging by the numbers they brought in just this year alone though, they had the potential to be even bigger. Teaming up with some of the local restaurants and stores in L.A., they were really moving way smarter than I thought. They actually had people delivering food along with a little nose candy.

"Fe, inside the app we created, I was able to sneak a secret menu option in, black market style. I designed it with my boy's firewall protection software plus all of latest spyware. It's not traceable, sis."

I was so hesitant as I looked at my brother standing here intelligent and grown as ever. I didn't wanna put him in this lifestyle, but this was some next level shit. This could be huge, and I wanted in.

"This is crazy, little brother. This could be really big. I wanna help you, but I don't want you losing sight of finishing school. I actually wanna take this off your hands all together, but I know that it wouldn't be fair to you."

"Look, sis, I'm not forgetting about school. This shit ain't gon' make me not want my education anymore. If anything, it's making me more eager to graduate."

"…and this friend you talking about, you trust him?" I asked, handing him the folder back.

"I mean, B, he cool. He fronted the money for us to get everything started," he replied nonchalantly.

My brother never had the best opinions when it came to the word "friends." Growing up, he always brought around a bunch of weird, fake-ass, thugs, so I knew I couldn't trust his judgment on this.

"Whatever he fronted, I'll get the money for him, but we don't do business with outsiders. I'm going to talk to Jacari about plugging you, but, baby brother, we finna set shit on fire with this shit."

CHAPTER FOURTEEN

Sitting in my office, I came up with a little business plan of my own. I wanted to buy four 7-Eleven stores around the Bay Area. Most of the time, when you entered one of these stores, you're greeted by people of many different colors but almost never black…at least, where I'm from. I needed to have full-control of the store's operations if I wanted my plan to work though.

As I sat thinking hard on the ideas I had for Adam's business, like a lightbulb in my brain, an idea struck. If executed correctly, this could possibly change the game.

Logging into my computer, I immediately Google searched diversion cans. With our app being completely on the black market and discreet, this would allow our users to locate cocaine at the hands of their phones. The special orders would be concealed as regular items stocked in the store that would be easy to find. They could either pick-up or have the items delivered. Of course, with the delivery service, we were going to actually need to partner with other restaurants as my brother had; this plan seemed bulletproof.

After finishing up the proposal, I sat back and smiled to myself. This shit was finna make me a whole lot of money. I was already thinking of ways to invest and give back to the community like Tristan would have wanted me to. I knew I could've already been doing so, but with this kind of money, I could help out a bunch of hoods in need.

As I finally decided to focus on my real job that I was here to get paid to do, my mind was in overdrive. We had a big meeting tomorrow with Sam's Club that I wasn't too confident about. They were looking to turn all their registers into virtual check stands, requesting talkback features, and a holographic face presence. I didn't know if I was up for the task. A lot would be riding on this. It would be huge for my company, but it was going to be a lot of work, and I would need the full commitment of all of my developers. We would have to work together, but if we did it right, we'd have every major company ringing our phones off the hook.

Since Tristan's death, the thought of opening up my own company had been weighing heavily on my mind. I'd been on the fence about it because the start of any business is a gamble, but life was short, and I learned that you have to go after what you want. I was definitely going to at least stick around for this Sam's Club project, but after everything was done with, I planned to give Brian my official notice of resignation. This job had been such a huge stepping stone for me, but when it's time to say goodbye, it's just time.

If everything went well, I'd be parting ways with a big sum of money but also setting this company up to continue thriving. Everybody wins.

For the rest of the day, I worked tirelessly on the PowerPoint to present for tomorrow's meeting. My eyes were starting to get heavy when I finally decided that I'd just finish at home.

As I rode the elevator down to meet my security, I thought about how Shanice, Janae, and I had bonded so much over the past few months. One day, I got them to hit the weed, and we just sat and talked for hours. Whenever I needed to vent, they were always waiting with listening ears and understanding hearts. The bond that we built only solidified my expectations. They were the best of the best, and I couldn't imagine any other women protecting me. I knew that if shit got real, with no hesitation, they would guard me with their lives. That alone made them feel like family to me, and I made sure we had dinner together often like one.

I'd given Adam the money to pay off his friend, so that they were square biz, and everything could be put into motion. We didn't need any unknowns involved in this, and his friend was a liability.

Adam left late last night to return to campus and break the news to his friend. I really needed him to focus on graduating, but that didn't mean he couldn't help me grow a business as well. I just truly hoped I wasn't making a huge mistake by allowing him into this lifestyle.

As we drove down the 580 freeway on the way to my new two-bedroom small house, all I could think about was this business. My brother came up with the new name *Speedy,* and I loved it. Our service and new app launch was about to be wild.

Reaching into my purse to pull out my phone, I spotted the card that the man from the Money Room had given me. That night at the lounge seemed so long ago, but the effects he had on my body still felt fresh. It seemed like it had been years since anyone had touched me sexually, and he did something to me without even using his hands.

Interrupting me from my naughty thoughts, my phone rang with the signature Apple ringtone. It was Mikel.

"What bitch?" I answered playfully with the phone on speaker and my head resting against the seat. We were about to exit off the freeway on Hesperian Boulevard, and I couldn't wait to get home.

"Come to the shop, hoe...let me hook up them weeds you've been letting grow all wild over yo' head," he said, referring to my natural hair that I'd been trying to manage but had been failing miserably at. I tried to wear it curly, but it was cute one day and a puffball the next. So, it always ended up in a bun or ponytail.

"I'm just about to pull into my driveway. I don't feel like comin' back out," I whined, "You might as well just come on over and work yo' magic while we sip some and smoke some like we usually do."

"Dumb bitch, you know I can't turn down no liquor. I'm on my way, hoe, and whatever my hands feel like doin', they doin'." Hanging up the phone in my face, he had the girls and me cracking up. Now, they knew just like I did how crazy his ass was.

"Y'all see what I go through? Anybody looking for a new best friend?" I asked, leaning up as I looked between the two of them.

"Girl, bye...you know you wouldn't trade his looney-ass for nobody," Janae said as she looked back at me, laughing lightly.

"You right, you right. The nigga works my last nerve, but there's never been a time that he wasn't there for me...anyway, y'all tryna come in and smoke? I know y'all ain't got shit else to do," I replied, playfully copying Smokey's voice from the movie *Friday.*

Looking at each other questionably, they both shrugged their shoulders in unison before following me inside. As we entered, they took in the decor because I finally finished setting up my new living room. A huge painted portrait of me and Tristan's very first photo together hung over the fireplace. A local street artist wanted to charge me next to nothing, but I paid him graciously for it.

After grabbing the blunts from my back room, I poured us all a glass of Stella Rosa Sweet Red wine.

"Here she go...tryna get us fucked up again," Shanice whispered to Janae as they both busted out laughing.

When I first hired them, they were so reserved and quiet, but the weed be letting you know. I stayed persistent in offering them to smoke or drink with me, and, finally, their wannabe G.I. Joe asses agreed. We'd been swapping stories and talking shit to each other ever since.

Walking into the door with a stank look on his face like always, Mikel was feeling territorial. He could tell how close the girls and I were getting, and he didn't like it. In his eyes, there could only be one.

"What the fuck are the wannabe FBI doing inside? Damn, bitch, you was that lonely that you couldn't wait to talk to me? I'm here now, raggedies...y'all can be gone," he told them, pulling his salon supplies in behind him. His ass hadn't even been in the door five-whole-minutes, and, already, he was starting some shit.

"Kel, leave them the fuck alone. I invited them inside for a session, and they're welcome to stay however long they want." Cutting my eyes at him, I finally lit the tip of the blunt I was holding before inhaling deeply.

With his head tilted slightly to the side, Mikel looked at me as if he didn't know who I was. Standing there squinting, he rolled his eyes so hard that I was sure the nigga had a headache before pulling his stuff into my room.

Looking over at the girls, we all broke out in silent laughter as I passed the blunt to Shanice. Standing up, I motioned for them to follow me to the room, knowing that it was gonna work Mikel's nerves.

"Uh uhh, bitch, quit playing. You know I don't like a lot of people around while I'm tryna do hair."

Ignoring him just like I told them to do, Janae went over and handed him the blunt while smiling. Looking at her face, Kel tried his best to keep the mug he had on but ended up smiling and laughing to himself. Janae just had one of those smiles that drew people to her.

With one of my dining room table chairs positioned in front of my wide bathroom mirror, we all sat and smoked as Mikel started on my hair.

In the short few months Shanice and Janae had been working for me, I managed to learn so much about them. They'd been friends for over ten-years and were both 24. They were born and raised in Oakland like Tristan was, and, in a few ways, they acted crazy like he did too. The Town could easily make or break people, but both of them had defied all odds. They'd recently graduated and received their college degrees—Shanice with an Associates in Journalism and Janae with a Master's in Business. I hadn't even known them that long, and, still, I was proud of them. Anybody who could make something out of themselves from nothing deserved recognition.

"Janae, girl, who got you over there cheesing hard as fuck in yo' phone like that? Aww, I remember that feeling," I told her as memories of the butterflies I used to get when texting or talking to Tristan came to mind.

"Oh, you know, just one of my lil' baes or whateva," she chuckled, texting rapidly, only looking up for a split-second.

Smiling to myself, I thought about the possibility of being with another man, and the thought alone caused a pain in my heart. Would it truly be possible for me to ever love again? Tristan had my heart and soul, but, now, he was ten-feet under. I wouldn't be able to love again without my heart. Tristan was my soulmate, and as far as I knew, you only get one of those.

My thoughts were causing my mood to shift downhill, but, luckily, Mikel snapping loud as shit in my ear pulled me from my pity party.

"Turn yo' head to the left, bitch, before I pop you like yo' mama used to," he said as he held the comb back really ready to pop my ass, causing everyone to laugh.

The hours seemed to be just flying by, but my ass was starting to feel numb from sitting in the wooden chair for so long. When Kel finally put the last curl in my head, Shanice and Janae were lying on the bed as I stood up and took in the look. The extensions were jet-black fading to fire red at the tips, and I was in love. The side part and the way my bestie had slayed my curls to perfection had me doing the "weave dance." I was feeling the fuck outta myself and couldn't nobody tell me shit as I stood in the mirror snapping selfies.

"Alright, let me stop fucking around. I know y'all staying 'cause it's late as fuck, and I don't wanna hear shit else. Couch or office? Y'all choose," I told Shanice and Janae before walking to my hall closet to grab blankets for them.

"I'll just gon' head and sleep on the couch. All Janae goofy-ass finna be doing is cupcaking all night," Shanice said as we all laughed way too hard, knowing she was telling the truth. Janae hadn't put her phone down yet.

After climbing into a quick shower and putting my bonnet on, I got in my bed and was out before my head had even touched the pillow.

Dalanna Anitra

A few hours later, I was woken up by the sound of my phone vibrating on the nightstand. I patiently waited for the person to stop calling me when finally I snatched the phone to see who the fuck was blowing me up. It was from a number I didn't even recognize, and I was pissed. They'd been calling me nonstop, and I was truly getting madder every time.

Angrily, I finally accepted the call.

"Hel-," I started to say, but before I could even fully get the word out of my mouth, a male voice took over.

"Fe, it's Boogie. Cari got hit up last night. Shit ain't looking good, ma. He's at Highland Hospital," he spoke in a pained tone. Boogie ran shit out in San Jo, but he and Jacari were tight. The sadness I heard in his voice caused me to think that Cari may have already been dead.

"Okay, say no more. I'll be up there as soon as I can," I told him, trying to keep my voice stable as I ended the call.

130

CHAPTER FIFTEEN

Walking down a long hallway inside the freezing cold hospital, I was headed to the waiting room where Jacari's family and friends were as I said a silent prayer. After losing Tristan and all the chaos that happened at his funeral, I thought the bullshit was finally over, but, really, it had just begun.

As I entered into the small room, all eyes turned to me filled with eagerness. Everyone was waiting to hear something. I'm sure they were expecting it to be a doctor with some news. The look of disappointment that spread across everyone's face caused me to feel bad that I had nothing to tell them.

As I stood at the entrance scanning the room, I found Boogie seated in a chair close to the wall with blood red eyes. He was zoned, out looking like he was ready to kill a nigga until I came and sat next to him.

"What happened, Boog?" I wasted no time with small talk and got straight to the point.

"Man, we were leaving out of New Karibbean City in the Town, and he saw some bitch he knew. We were already hella on. I tried to tell the nigga to be cool. The bitch was already boo'd up with some nigga who had his boys behind him, so I knew it was gon' be some drama. I kept on tryna tell brah not to go over there, but he insisted that he knew her and that he wasn't tryna talk to her like that. He was on and started pushing me, so I just let him go. I fired up a blunt and leaned against my car as I watched him approach them. He was callin' her name out hella loud, and from the look on her dude's face, I could tell it was fa sho finna be a problem. He probably saw it too, but you know Cari wasn't finna back down. He approached her, and I put my hand on my burner just in case. Still getting high though, I watched as he pulled her in for a hug when the dude whipped out his hammer and let two off. The shit happened so fast, Fe. I didn't even have a chance to react. I knew some shit was finna go down, and I should've been ready, but I never expected shit to go down like that. I should've had his back." Remorse filled his eyes before he covered his face with his hands. I could tell that this whole situation was really weighing on Boogie.

Quickly rubbing my hand over his back, we just waited to find out Jacari's fate.

Looking around the room at all of Cari's family and friends, I was honestly a little resentful. Tristan never had a chance to fight or make it to the hospital. He was just dead. I knew that it wasn't the fault of anyone in the room, but, still, anger filled my heart. I knew this shit wouldn't be easy, but I didn't think mothafuckas would make it this hard either. Cari was my right-hand, the only nigga I trusted with everything out of all of Tristan's men. If he was gone, I didn't know what the fuck I was gonna do. The stress of not knowing was really just driving us all crazy.

After many hours had passed, a tall blonde white doctor entered the room causing almost everyone to immediately stand up.

"Are you all here for Jacari Thomas?" she asked plainly before Cari's mom spoke up.

"Yes, we are. How is he?"

"Well, Mrs. Thomas, your son was shot twice. One of the bullets entered in through the side of his abdomen, and the other entered in through his right chest cavity. We were able to locate and remove both bullets. Although, we did have some complications during surgery, your son's a fighter, and he pulled through. I can allow you to see him once he's inside of a room; however, he's been through a very extensive surgery, so we'll all be on-call to monitor him throughout the night. With time though, I do expect that he'll make a full recovery."

"Thank you, Lord! Thank you! Hallelujah!" Jacari's mom rejoiced with a huge grin on her face.

Shit, I felt like rejoicing my-damn-self because even though he'd be out the game for a while to recover, he was alive.

After saying my goodbyes to everyone and making sure to let Jacari's mama know that if she needed anything, I was only a call away, I headed downstairs. Janae and Shanice were patiently waiting, and as I approached them, I couldn't help but smile.

"Damn, y'all bitches waited this long? Y'all better than me. Even I would have left my ass," I told them while giggling to myself. They were as loyal as they came.

"Oh, naw, boss lady, we actually just pulled back up," Shanice said as they both started laughing.

"Yeah, we went to Popeye's," Janae added.

"Y'all annoying asses could have waited for me to go get food," I said, playfully rolling my eyes in annoyance.

After everything Boogie had told me, I couldn't help but feel like all this led back to Josiah. Was the bitch Cari was tryna speak to Talia? And, did she really let shit go down like that?

Taking my phone from out of my purse, I dialed Nalia with no hesitation. I was kind of assuming that she wouldn't answer since we hadn't spoken much lately, but she did.

"Hey, Fe," she spoke, sounding better than the last time I talked to her.

"Hey, Li, you busy? I wanted to run something by you."

"Bitch, no. My ass is at home Netflix and Chillin'. What's up?" she asked curiously.

"Do you know if Talia was at New Karribean last night?" I questioned as the phone got awkwardly quiet.

"This feels like it just turned into an interrogation, Fe. What's really up?" she replied, getting a bit defensive.

"Jacari was shot last night, and word was that he was just saying 'hi' to a female friend. Not trying to interrogate you, but I am trying to put all the pieces together," I told her honestly.

"Yeah, I mean, she was there, Fe. She invited me to come and said she'd introduce me to some of Josiah's friends, but I wasn't feeling it. She's been acting too damn dick dizzy, and if any of his niggas packing that kind of dick, I don't want it," she said, causing me to burst out laughing, but I knew she was dead-ass serious.

"Well, I know you will always be loyal to yo' sister, but I still need that job done if you're up for it. If you can figure out a way to get her away from Josiah and handle it, I promise you ain't gon' need to work again for a minute." I was propositioning her with an offer that hopefully she couldn't refuse.

As silence once again filled the phone, I waited for her response.

"I think I might have a plan...after this shit, I'm vacationing on somebody's fucking island. I'll handle it, Fe, and let you know when it's done," she spoke confidently, causing me to smile. It would only be a matter of time before Josiah's brains were being spilled somewhere, and as bad as I wanted to be the one to pull trigger, just the satisfaction of knowing that he'd no longer be breathing was enough for me.

After ending my call with Nalia, I was ready to just go straight home, but I needed to make a stop for wine first. It'd been so long since I'd actually cooked anything, so I figured I might as well pick up a few things to make dinner too.

Arriving at the Safeway that was conveniently located right around the corner from my new house, I took in my surroundings. The area was so diverse, and I loved it. I had no desire to be the only black person in a neighborhood full of white people.

I offered for the girls to come inside with me, but they declined because they wouldn't be able to take their guns. As I entered the store and grabbed a basket, I shook my head at their crazy asses. They always swore some shit was finna pop off.

Wearing an old pair of gray drawstring sweats and a white shirt that had the word *Original* written across it, I was comfy as fuck as I guided my cart to the meat section. My hair was lightly blowing behind me as I briskly walked down the aisle to get to the back of the store. I couldn't wait to go home and cook. I was planning to make salmon, sautéed spinach with onions, and garlic mashed potatoes. My stomach growled loudly just at the thought of a homecooked meal.

Walking over to the butcher, I requested two wild caught salmon fillets and a pound of jumbo shrimp.

"Damn, I ain't even hit yet, and I could spot that ass anywhere," a familiar mellow voice spoke from behind me.

Turning around, I came face-to-face with Mr. Seth Bivens—the man from the club who had my panties wet just from the sight of him. Much like our last encounter, my words were caught in my throat as I just stared at him admiringly. He was wearing an all-gray formfitting Under Amor shirt that made every muscle on his torso bulge out. As if the shirt didn't already have my mouth watering enough, he paired it with black and gray track pants that had a bulge of their own. I couldn't take my eyes off the print of his thick manhood until he cleared his throat, causing my eyes to meet his once again. I couldn't even remember what he had just said as we stood in awkward silence.

"So, yeah, like I was saying…you should let me cook that for you," he said as I listened intently, trying to stay focused on his eyes and not look at his dick.

"Now, why would I let some random-ass dude cook for me when I can just as easily do it myself?" I snapped back, trying to get smart to hide the fact that he had my honey pot leaking once again.

Maneuvering my cart, I tried to move around him and continue my shopping, but he just kept walking beside me.

"Well, for starters…'cause a nigga can cook," he said animatedly, causing me to chuckle, "And, secondly, 'cause from the way you was just staring at my dick, I know you wanna get to know me just as bad as I wanna get to know you, so don't fight the feeling. Let me take you out to dinner or at least make you dinner. Hell, we can do whatever you want as long as I get to see you again."

As we turned up the juice aisle, I tried to look anywhere else but at him and his smooth chocolate skin.

"Uhh, I…," I stammered before taking a deep breath and collecting my thoughts. "I love pasta," I managed to get out, shrugging my shoulders.

Once I looked his way again, I couldn't help but laugh at the confused look on his face. I was being so awkward, but, luckily, that was the ice breaker.

"I'm sorry. I didn't mean to be so weird. I'd love to go out to dinner with you, and I really do love pasta." Laughing awkwardly, I managed to pick out an Ocean Spray White Cran-Peach juice and placed it inside my basket. "You can pick the place. I'm too indecisive, so your idea, your plans. Let me see your phone."

Turning around to face him, I stared into his bedroom eyes, holding my hand out as a huge grin formed on his handsome face.

"Damn, that just made dick even harder. I love that bossy shit." Coming close to my ear, he spoke in a tone that made me wanna knock hella juices down and fuck him right there on aisle five.

Taking a few steps back, he wore a smirk that said he knew exactly what he was doing as I stored my number in his phone.

"So, I guess I'll let you finish shopping, and I'll hit you up later?"

"Yeah, that's cool. I'll be looking forward to it. I mean, not like waiting…but, yeah, that's fine," I said, letting my thoughts get the best of the conversation.

My nerves and overthinking caused both of us to just walk off with him pointing to his phone, signaling that he'd hit me up before he bent the corner.

Once I could breathe again, a giddy smile spread across my face. Even though I was still mourning

Tristan's death, I needed to know that I could feel normal again, that I was capable of starting over without him. I just needed to feel something other than numbness, and Seth did exactly that for me. I wasn't expecting to fall in love with him, but I did want to get to know him better and see where this led.

*****

As we pulled into my driveway, the giddiness I was feeling instantly faded. Sitting in his car with some nerd-looking-ass nigga was Adam who was wearing a stupid look on his face as he watched us pull in. Getting out at the same time, we both rounded the back of our cars before meeting on the sidewalk.

"Just hear him out, Fe. I promise you I wouldn't've brought him here if this wasn't something I thought you needed to hear."

Blowing out an irritated sigh, I rolled my eyes and tried to fix the huge attitude that was brewing. I couldn't believe he brought this fool to my house.

"You know I don't like weird shit. You could've just called, Adam. Jacari was shot yesterday, and there's been hella shit going on. I really don't have time for this."

"Well, sounds like now's the perfect time for you to hear my boy out."

"Y'all got 15-20-minutes max. Let's go."

Quickly turning on my heels, I grabbed my bags from the car before entering the house.

After putting away all my groceries, I took a seat on the couch as I impatiently waited for them to come inside. Adam entered first and following behind him was his light-skin lanky friend, carrying some sort of briefcase as they came and stood before me. Being the goofy little brother that I knew him to be, Adam couldn't keep a straight face as he came and plopped down on the couch next to me.

"Tell her what you got to say, brah," he said as my eyes shifted from him back to his friend.

Stepping up, he set the briefcase down onto my coffee table before opening it up, revealing what looked to be a drone of some sort as I looked at my brother in confusion.

"So, my name is Bernard, and I designed this drone with the same underground technology that I developed and used in the software for the app Adam and I were previously using. This drone is completely untraceable and has an impressive range of up to 500-miles. It flies low enough to where it wouldn't be detected on any radar. It's super badass, and it's also only the beginning of what we've been creating. We have our take on new age vending machines, diversion cans, and my boys and I have even been engineering a self-driving car. I'm here because Adam and I agreed that maybe I'd be more useful being a part of the team than being paid out."

Standing in front of me, he powered the drone on and grabbed a small tablet that still lay flat in the briefcase. After powering it on and pressing a few things, he handed it over to me with a camera monitor displaying on half the screen. There was also a small map in the corner. The other half of the tablet was where the drone's controls were located, and I just wanted to see what it could do already. Because we were inside, I could only see the floor, but I had to admit that I was definitely impressed.

"Wow, I've never actually played with one of these before," I told them as a wide smile came over my face.

139

Taking the drone and the tablet, I walked out into my backyard as they followed behind me.

"Let me just quickly show you, and then I'll let you get your wings."

Walking over to me, Bernard grabbed the drone and pressed a button before placing it on the ground. That caused the bottom motors to start rotating, and the drone's propellers started spinning. Eagerly, I watched as he used the controls to slowly bring it off the ground and brought it into the air. He navigated it up so that it was hovering slightly above my house. On the tablet, you could now see us standing on patio. Standing beside him, I was watching his every move, and he knew because he finally handed me the tablet.

Looking over at my baby brother, I grinned as I carefully maneuvered the drone through the sky.

"Quit being a nerd and acting all scared. Mob that shit!" Adam playfully shouted, causing me to chuckle lightly.

"You ain't said shit but a word, nigga."

Pressing down on the control, I watched as the speed increased. Everything on the camera was moving so fast, and before I knew it, I was going the max speed of 75 m.p.h. I was in love with this thing and didn't even need to see anymore. Bernard had proven that he'd be a useful asset to me in less than ten-minutes.

"Okay, that's it. I'm sold. Give me my money back, chump, and you can be a part of the new business," I told Bernard as I handed him the tablet back.

"Money? What money?" he asked, genuinely confused before I looked over at Adam. He was trying to contain his laughter before he exploded and grabbed his stomach in pain as he laughed heartily. Him thinking this shit was a game allowed me to take off running towards him. Before I could reach him though, he stopped laughing and took off too. Finally catching up to him, I was just about to punch the shit out of him when he stopped me.

"Sis, we just added another way for delivery to our service. Why you being all mean?"

"Fuck that, nigga. 'Bout my paper, you gots to see me."

CHAPTER SIXTEEN

Rising from the deep slumber I was in, I checked my phone, and a huge smile spread across my face. A text message from Seth had already brightened my day, and I'd just woken up. It was just a simple *good morning,* but it gave me a feeling that I hadn't experienced in a while—*excitement.* I was so juiced to see that I was the first thing on his mind this early, and a goofy smile was planted on my face as I quickly replied.

The weekend had approached, and I was in such a good mood knowing that it was Friday. Our meeting with Sam's Club had been delayed until today, and as good as I was feeling, I didn't have any doubt that this meeting was going to be a success.

Finally getting out of the bed, I hurried to shower and finish my morning hygiene so that I wouldn't be late. I was moving so rapidly around the room all the while texting Seth as well. Looking down at my phone, I applied a quick coat of lipstick and was all smiles as I read the new message. Seth had all the same qualities that Tristan did, and, honestly, that scared me a little. He appeared to be both book and street smart. He was fine and possessed this cocky smile that let me know he had bitches at his fingertips. A bunch of his traits were red flags too though. I probably should have ran the other way, but I couldn't tear my eyes from the phone as we engaged in what would be the first of many cupcake sessions.

Grabbing my purse, I headed for the door as a FaceTime call came through on my phone.

"I was tired of not being able to see that pretty-ass face of yours," Seth spoke as his face appeared on the screen, causing me to blush. "What you got going for the day?" he asked as he placed the camera down, making sure that I could still see him before bringing a white doctor's coat over his shoulders.

"You did not tell me that you were a doctor."

"Well, you didn't ask either. But, since we're on the topic...I'm actually a neonatal surgeon at Children's Hospital. You look like you're on your way to work as well though, right? What's the mystery job?"

Picking his phone back up, he waited for my reply as I climbed into the backseat and greeted the ladies "good morning."

"So, I'm actually the president of an IT firm. My company and I design, engineer, and manufacture software and applications for businesses. Not as good as saving babies, but you know...I do a lil' something," I said, holding the phone up to my face.

"Oh, it sounds like you do more than a lil' something. As a black woman in today's society, that sounds like a *huge* accomplishment. A black woman running an IT company? Girl, you are amazing." He genuinely looked impressed.

"Well, thank you, Mr. Bivens. You being a black male surgeon is also a major accomplishment, and as if just being a surgeon wasn't enough, you're a surgeon who saves babies! Hell, you're a modern-day Superman, just your cape is white instead of red. So, you're pretty damn amazing yourself," I told him as I reached over to pick up a blunt before setting my phone down to light it.

"Aww, shit, you tryna make a brotha blush," he joked. "So, you smoke, huh?" he asked, noticing the smoke that quickly filled the backseat.

"Yes, sir," I told him as I blew the smoke into the camera of my phone. "I know a lot of men find it unattractive, but I *un*apologetically smoke my weed. So, if it's a turnoff or something for you, let's definitely get that out into the open now," I said, looking into the phone as I continued to smoke.

"No judgement on my side, Ms. Felicia. Shit, I like to smoke a joint or eat an edible every now and then too," he spoke honestly.

"*Ooooh,* you can't be a doctor *and* like weed," I told him childishly.

"Bullshit. Weed has made a huge impact on the world medically, therefore giving us doctors the greenlight to use it for both our patients and ourselves," he chuckled.

"You're just an open book, aren't you?"

"Yep…anything you wanna know."

"Okay, so when's this date supposed to be happening, and how you doing on the planning side?"

"I'm actually glad you asked 'cause I was gonna bring that up as well. Are you free tonight? I found the perfect little Italian restaurant in San Francisco, and we can eat *all* the pasta you want."

"Wasting no time, huh? Well, I honestly wasn't gonna do shit later but go home and watch *Insecure* on HBO, but that sounds way better. Pasta and hopefully chocolate for dessert? I'm down," I told him as I put the blunt I'd been smoking out as we pulled into the parking garage of my office building.

"Does 8 o'clock work for you?"

"That's perfect."

"A'ight, well, I can't wait to see you, beautiful. Enjoy your day, and I'll see you at 8 p.m."

"Okay, you enjoy your day as well...see you later. Bye," I said sweetly as I ended the FaceTime call. I was cheesing so hard that my cheeks were hurting.

"Okay, bitch, get yo' groove back then," Janae said as I excited the car, cracking up and waving goodbye.

As I entered the building and rode the elevator upstairs, I pulled out my roll-on Calvin Klein perfume and quickly applied some to my wrists and behind my ears. When the doors opened, I was applying another quick coat of lipstick before walking out. Making my way to the conference room, I went over my speech in my head as confirmation that I had everything down. Once I entered the room, everyone got eerily quiet as they all turned their attention to me.

"Thank you all for being here. I hope you weren't waiting too long. I won't waste time with small talk but instead get right down to business. The first slide is a prototype that I designed just to give you guys a feel for how the actual registers will look. I named the virtual checker 'Amy.' She is very intelligent and is programed to answer product information as well."

As I continued my slideshow, I presented them with the software behind Amy and how her voice would actually sound. I also was able to provide them with an example of how their customers would check their items out and have the option to make small talk with Amy. After presenting the last slide, the whole room erupted in applause. Making my way around the room, I shook hands with everyone and thanked them.

As I reached the CEO of Sam's Club Mr. John Furner, he looked at me with amazement in his eyes.

"You are truly outstanding, Felicia. We are going to be able to provide our customers with an experience they'll never forget. If this is pulled off smoothly, I'm going to be personally recommending you to a bunch of my friends and fellow colleagues."

"Wow, sir, that is awesome. I only hope I meet all of your expectations."

"I have no doubt that you will, Felicia. Don't work too hard now," he said as he made his way out of the conference room with his team.

Now sitting in the room alone, I exhaled as I looked out at the City with pride. I had accomplished so much to just be a small-time girl from a big city.

*****

On my way home from the office, I texted Mikel *911,* signaling that there was an emergency and for him to meet me at my house. I sat patiently, waiting for him to enter because I knew it wouldn't be long before he did. *911* texts were only to be used if one of us was in some serious shit, but, in this case, I just wanted a new hairstyle for my date tonight.

Scrolling through my phone, I rolled my eyes at all the silly hoes on Facebook singing the same old tune. These bitches swore somebody either wanted to be them or wanted their man.

Bitch, you don't even wanna be you or want yo' own man. Laughing out loud to myself made me wish Kel would hurry his ass up.

Just as the thought crossed my mind, I heard my door open and footsteps rapidly approaching.

"…oh, no, bitch, this bet not be no fucking game. You don't look distraught or like shit is wrong with you,"

146

he spoke out of breath, which caused me to start dying laughing. My bestie was a true ride or die 'cause the nigga had really been rushing to get over here.

"I'm sorry, best friend. It's not a *real* emergency, but I do have a date tonight. The red's been cool, but I want something that says, 'I'm a boss-ass bitch, and you'd be a fool not to take me home,'" I told him as I got up to look at my reflection in the mirror.

"What time is the date? And who's it with?" he asked dryly.

"8 p.m. and the guy from the club…Seth. He slipped me his card before we left that night. Then, I ran into him again at Safeway, and we've been texting and facetiming ever since. He invited me out to dinner tonight, and I'm nervous as fuck. I need everything to be perfect. I don't wanna give him any reason to run from me. With everything I have going on with being in the game now, I just don't wanna give out any impression that I'm a dangerous person. I want him to just look at me like I'm the most beautiful woman in the room."

"Okay, Cinderella, you know I got you. We don't gotta lot of time though, so go grab a chair, so we can get started."

By the time we were finished, it was 7 o'clock, and I had to rush to get ready. Luckily, while I was taking a quick shower, Mikel picked out an all-black, formfitting, dress that stopped at my knees and had a deep v-cut. He paired it with a black leather jacket and my black Louboutin pumps.

"Ugh, what would I do without you?" I asked Mikel as I quickly made my way over to the bed where he had the outfit laid out and began to get dressed.

"Ya' life would be miserable as shit without me, hoe, so don't even think about that…just thank me," he said cockily as he rolled his eyes and smiled.

Looking in the mirror, you would think I'd went on somebody's makeover show. In just a few hours, my whole look had changed. Mikel turned my long red extensions into a jet-black bob with feathered bangs. All of my assets were on full display, and I was definitely hoping that Seth would take me home tonight. The way my pussy has been throbbing…shit, I'd jump on his dick in the bathroom if need be. I was horny, and Seth needed to fulfil my desires.

"Get out the mirror, bitch. You gon' be late," Mikel said, holding a black and red Chanel bag for me take.

Walking over to him, I quickly grabbed it before taking a look inside. Kel made sure my phone, lipstick, bobby pins, and everything else that I'd needed were inside.

After saying a quick "goodbye," I rushed out to the car, so that I wouldn't be late.

The ride seemed to be taking forever, so I texted Seth and let him know that I was on my way, but that I would possibly be a bit late.

Finally arriving at the restaurant almost an hour later, I nervously got out and waved goodbye to my security. Standing on the sidewalk, I took a deep breath before slowly exhaling it, trying to calm my nerves.

Just as I was about to walk inside, I heard his voice from behind me.

"Damn, girl, you look amazing. I almost don't want you to turn around though 'cause that ass is looking way too good," he spoke, walking up to me as he pulled me in for a brief hug.

"Stop it…you gassing me right now," I told him as he held his arm out for me to take and led the way inside.

As we entered the restaurant, I was puzzled because there was no one inside. The place was completely empty on a Friday night.

"Mr. Bivens, I presume?" a hostess asked, appearing at the podium to take us to our seats.

Looking over at Seth who couldn't hide his smile, I knew that he'd planned this.

We were guided into the dining area where a lone candle was lit on each table surrounding ours which had two long candles of its own flickering under the dim lighting.

"My father always told me that first impressions are everything. I know this *technically* isn't our first encounter, but it is our first date, and I wanted to make it memorable."

"This is beautiful. I'm honestly a little speechless," I told him as we took our seats.

"Well, then, my mission has been accomplished. I know you said all this date needed to include was pasta, but I thought I'd take things a little step further. Plus, this is honestly only the beginning of our night."

"Just full of surprises, huh? Okay. I won't ask any questions. I'll just follow your lead."

"The way you said that shit made my dick hard. Damn, hold up," he said as he stood up and adjusted his pants before sitting back down. I couldn't help but smile watching him sweat a little. "We might not make it through dinner if you keep on tryna seduce me like this."

"Boy, I didn't even do nothing," I laughed. "And, where in the hell are our menus? Nigga, you done bought the restaurant out but didn't buy the service?" I asked jokingly, but I was dead-ass serious.

"Ay, you need to chill. You must ain't had no dick in a minute, huh? You tense as hell...we don't have any menus 'cause I told them that we wanted to try every pasta they had on the menu. Yo' ass just said pasta, so, tonight, we feastin'."

Sitting on the opposite side of the table, I just stared at him as my pussy started to get wet. He was so damn sweet and was looking all debonair sitting across from me wearing a black button-up dress shirt with black slacks to match. Around his neck was a Cuban link gold chain that he paired with a gold Rolex. His chocolate-ass knew he was looking good enough to eat, and I was fighting to contain myself. I was about ready to tell him to meet me in the bathroom when the waiter approached our table with a basket of warm bread sticks and a bottle of champagne on ice.

"The first dish will be out in just a few moments. We are starting things off with our Penne San Remo. It's angel hair pasta, chicken breast, artichoke hearts, sun dried tomatoes, and peas with a white wine cream sauce."

"That sounds so good," I said before he made his way back to the kitchen. "How was your day today? I know you got a good baby saving story for me," I chuckled as I grabbed a piece of bread and ripped off a small piece before placing it in my mouth.

"Surprisingly, I have no real interesting stories. I was only scheduled for one surgery today, and it was canceled; the mother got cold feet, so I just spent the rest of the day on-call. What about you? Any interesting tech stories?" he asked, smiling slightly as he grabbed the bottle of champagne and filled both of our glasses.

"Nothing too interesting either. I just had a meeting with Sam's Club, pitching my ideas on their new holographic check stand project. I presented them with a prototype, and…" Realizing that I was probably talking too much, I awkwardly exhaled before putting the last bite of bread into my mouth. "I'm sorry. I can get too caught up talking about my work sometimes, but, pretty much, I had a good meeting with Sam's Club," I told him once I finished chewing before taking a sip from my glass.

"Don't downplay your love for what you do. It's cool. I could listen to you talk all day honestly," he said, looking deep into my eyes, causing me to blush.

"Thank you," I replied sweetly.

The rest of our time at the restaurant was spent trying so many different pastas that I honestly lost count. They were going to continue bringing them, but I tapped out. Seth and I were both full as fuck. I knew he was just trying to keep going for my sake, so I spoke up for the both of us.

"No mas. No more. No more," I whined as I slightly slouched in my chair a bit. Sitting across from me, all Seth could do was laugh. My stomach was poking out from being so full, and I knew he probably wasn't expecting me to be so comfortable with him already.

"Don't be looking like you just caught the itis over there or some shit. I still got one more thing planned for us. You down?" he asked, standing up from the table with the candle lights flickering against his chocolate skin as he held his hand out for me to take.

"Nigga, I stay down. Let's go," I told him as I took his hand with a huge smile planted on my face.

CHAPTER SEVENTEEN

We rode in the back of an all-black town car headed for the next surprise. When we pulled into a small airport, I looked at Seth skeptically as a huge grin formed on his face. There was a private jet waiting for us, and my palms started to get sweaty as I thought about the possibility of getting on that plane.

I'd just met this man and already he was trying to take me on a trip. I hadn't called Mikel or anyone to let them know that we decided to extend our date, and, honestly, my nerves were getting the best of me.

What if this nigga is just tryna take me out the city so he can rape me or insert me into some wild sex trafficking shit? Any-fucking-thing could happen, I thought to myself, knowing that I was thinking way too hard.

My mind was running a mile a minute, and I'm sure Seth could tell by the puzzled look that was plastered on his face. He was saying something, but I was too wrapped up in my own thoughts to even hear him or respond.

Once I calmed myself down though, I realized that I was uneasy for no reason. There would be no raping going on 'cause I was ready and willing to throw my pussy at this nigga anyway.

"Miss I'm Always Down, you coming or what?" Seth asked as he exited the car and extended his hand for me to take again.

Walking across the pavement and onto the stairs of the jet, we walked hand-in-hand as I asked question after question about where the hell we were going. I didn't have any clothes or luggage. This whole thing was spontaneous as fuck, but I loved it.

"Brah, relax. Get out your head. We got 48-hours left to spend together. You'll know where we're going when we land," he said with finality, causing my kitty to jump as I nodded my head and shut the hell up.

Thirteen-hours later, we were hovering over Italy as I looked down at the beautiful scenery. It'd been so long since I traveled, and the views alone provided an antidote to the heartbreak I'd been feeling ever since Tristan's death.

With an almost empty glass of wine in hand, I gazed at the sun and just silently smiled to myself. I was happy I decided to come.

Sitting across from me, Seth was rapidly texting on his phone, and it had me wondering was he into something else.

I know doctors make bookoo bucks, but I didn't know they made private jet money, I thought to myself as I just watched his fine-ass deep in whatever conversation he was having.

"Welcome to Palermo," the pilot announced dryly before the door to the jet opened up.

Finally looking up from his phone, Seth smiled as he caught me staring. With all the doubts I initially had about coming, something about this just felt right. I mean, what could be wrong about getting dicked down in a foreign European city anyway? I was gonna enjoy this ride while it lasted, both literally and figuratively.

"Twenty-four hours to fuck some shit up in Italy? Perk up, nigga...let's go," I told him as I grabbed my purse and tossed my phone inside before walking off the plane, switching my hips extra hard knowing he was watching my ass bounce as I walked away. The sexual tension that had been burning between us since that day at the club was finally about to be put out. I didn't even care if we didn't get to do any sightseeing. As long as the nigga fucked me 'til my mouth was dry, I would be cool. My pussy was getting wet just thinking about him sliding his thick-ass dick inside of me.

"Look, I'm tired as shit. I don't plan on fucking shit up until I get at least an hour of sleep," he replied, catching up to me and breaking me from my erotic thoughts.

Looking over at him, I smiled mischievously.

"Yeah, okay, we'll see about all that," I replied goofily.

As we rode through the streets of Palermo, I was engaged in my phone uploading selfies to Instagram that I'd taken on the plane. Unexpectedly, Seth gently grabbed my thigh, causing me to look up from the bullshit I'd previously been doing. Wasting no time, he grabbed me by the nape of my neck before hungrily pulling me into him for a kiss that left me speechless. Our tongues seemed like they were dancing to a rhythm as I felt my body's heat rising. Before I knew it, he was gently caressing my breasts, and I was rubbing on his erect manhood that was now poking through the pants he wore. If I didn't pull away, I might have actually fucked this man in the backseat of this car.

"*Mmm,*" I moaned as I broke away from the kiss feeling a bit dirty as I wiped my mouth and repositioned myself back into the seat, sitting up straight. The rest of the ride was a silent one as I kept my eyes glued to the window and my legs crossed.

We arrived at the Grand Hotel Villa Igiea with a sexual tension so strong that I'm sure even the driver could feel it.

As we stepped out into the cool morning air, a light breeze brushed across my skin. We were so caught up earlier that I hadn't even noticed that our hotel was surrounded by water. The beautiful ancient-looking beige and brown building was neighbored by the port of the sea, and it was such an amazing sight to see.

Making our way to the entrance, I spotted small boats lined along the dock and made a mental note to come back out and look around some more.

"Welcome to the Grand Hotel," a woman spoke with a thick Italian accent as we approached the front desk. The marble flooring and high ceilings with extravagant chandeliers hanging gave the decor classic and memorable vibes.

After checking in, we were guided to our villa, and I couldn't help but think that this place just kept getting better and better.

Upon walking into the villa, the first thing I noticed was the wild-looking salmon-colored floral wallpaper. It followed the theme of the rest of the hotel, giving the room a timeless feel accompanied by a bit of modern-day style. However, I had to admit, I would not have personally chosen the color. The couches as well as the curtains were coordinated with the wallpaper, and it was all just a bit too much.

A lone huge flat screen hung on the wall, and a pretty dark-brown coffee table was centered in the middle of everything. As I made my way back into the bedroom, I noticed that more of the wallpaper covered the walls, but the ceiling was a bright white with an amazing skylight.

Mirrors were aligned across the wall near the bed, and there were double-doors revealing the patio.

Sliding the heels I'd been wearing off my feet, I walked out onto the balcony and got lost in the view. The way the sunshine reflected against the water had me in awe, and I just wanted to savor this moment of joyfulness.

Smelling his cologne before I actually felt his presence, Seth brought his arms around me as we looked out at the water together. I felt so safe in his arms and hadn't been held this way since Tristan passed. Trying not to become overwhelmed with emotion, I rested my head against his chest and just enjoyed the warmth that he provided me with.

Turning around to face him, I placed a sensual kiss on his lips before proceeding back inside. As I walked to the bedroom, I reached behind me to unzip the dress that I'd been waiting so long to desperately peel off. Easing it off of both shoulders, I let it fall to the ground before entering the bathroom. Standing in just the black and nude lingerie set that I'd chosen for our date, I turned the shower to steaming hot as I smiled to myself.

"I'm 'bout to fuck the shit out this nigga," I giggled lowly before Seth appeared in the doorway leaving my jaw on the floor. His thick wood was standing at a full attention as he stood there lustfully watching me undress. The way his shit curved inside the pants he was wearing caused my honey pot to runneth over as so many dirty thoughts ran through my mind. Biting my lip, I shyly turned away before grabbing an all-white face towel and a small fancy bar of soap as I entered into the steaming hot water. Through the glass, I could see Seth begin to undress as he pulled his shirt over his head first before dropping his pants and boxers as well. Standing there fully naked, even through the glass, I could see the rips in his muscular body, and that his dick was still rock hard as he approached the shower. Removing the wrapper from around the small bar of soap with an Italian name, I lathered my towel and began washing all over my body.

"Is it coo if I join you?" he asked, pulling the shower door open as I nodded my head, allowing him to come inside.

With my back turned to him, he walked up behind me before reaching around and wetting his face towel as his member poked against my butt cheeks begging for attention. Goosebumps rose on my skin as I nervously turned around and surrendered to the desire of needing to feel him inside me.

Reaching down, he wasted no time before he started rubbing my pussy and nipples simultaneously causing me to gasp loudly. Before my moans could get too out of control, I eagerly placed my lips to his and took the lead, stroking him long and slow. Placing my hand on his chest as our passionate kiss deepened, I lightly backed him into the wall before dropping to my knees. Using my tongue, I swirled around the head of his shaft as I looked up at him, never taking my eyes off his. Bringing him all the way into my mouth, I let all my nerves go down the drain. Placing a hand around the base of his dick, I started sucking and slurping loudly as my hands matched the movements of my mouth. I spotted Seth's toes curling and knew I was doing the damn thang as he tilted his head back before grabbing ahold of the wall for support.

"Goddamn, Fe," he moaned as I felt him grow just a little bit harder and knew he was getting ready to bust.

Pulling me up from off my knees, he brought my soaking wet body close to his with his arms tightly around my waist. Bringing his lips down to meet mine, he placed a delicate kiss on my lips before firmly smacking me on the ass, causing me to bury my face in his chest. Grabbing our face towels, we both lathered them once more before taking our time washing and caressing each other's bodies.

Being the first to step out, Seth grabbed himself a towel before holding one open for me to step out into and bringing it around me. Even after drying my body off, he still had me soaking wet and already feeling pure ecstasy. Unexpectedly, he picked me up off the ground as I screamed and resisted at first, but he assured me that he had me.

"Yo' ass ain't think a nigga was this strong, but chill. I'm not gon' drop you...relax and bring them legs around me," he commanded, and I gladly did as I was told.

Grabbing ahold of my ass cheeks, he walked us over to the bed before gently laying me down and dropping to his knees so that he was face-to-face with my neatly trimmed kitty. Sliding two fingers inside, he felt how wet I was before licking all my juices off his fingers and then proceeding to greedily suck and lick on my clit. Rubbing my nipples as I arched my back, loud moans escaped my mouth one after another. He had my body's heat rising so rapidly that I knew it wouldn't be long before he had my body trembling.

Bringing my swollen button into his mouth, he sucked sensuously, driving me crazy before he started flicking his tongue against it, and I couldn't hold back any longer.

"Fuck, I'm 'bout to cum!" I screamed before a wave of shocks caused my body to start twitching joyously. Biting down on my lip, I tried to control my screams until my body finally stopped trembling. Out of breath and with my eyes tightly closed, I opened them to see Seth admiring my body as he stroked his dick, causing my mouth to water. Standing up, I pushed him back onto the bed before stepping over him. Placing my hands on his chest, slowly, I brought my pussy down over his dick and allowed him inside of me. As he filled me up, I brought my head back in bliss before I started popping and twerking my shit up and down causing his eyes to roll back. I was hearing Tyga's hit song "Do My Dance" in my head as I moved my hips up and down, popping my ass and pussy hard, dropping down on him each time with more and more force. Reaching up, he played with my titties before closing his eyes as I continued to ride him effortlessly. Grabbing ahold of one of my cheeks, Seth came deep inside of me before flipping me over and entering right back into my pussy like he'd never left.

We spent the rest of the night exploring positions I didn't even know my body could get into and ended things off on the balcony with him pulling my hair and me throwing my ass back like it would be the last time we ever fucked.

Eventually, we made our way to the bed and sleep engulfed us as soon as our heads hit the pillows.

CHAPTER EIGHTEEN

I woke up the next morning and checked my phone to see that it had ten-missed calls and four text messages from Mikel. The texts were all him cussing me out for not picking up the phone. I was just about to reply when Seth started waking up beside me. Without opening his eyes, he felt for my body before finding my thigh and tugging at it, signaling that he wanted me to lay back down. Placing the phone back on the nightstand, I didn't protest as I slid my body back beside his and allowed him to wrap his arm around my waist.

Sightseeing had been the last thing on our minds. We were content where we were as we sat and watched TV, ordering way too much room service. I'd let him get some rest, but as soon as he was up, I had his dick in my mouth 'cause I needed him hard, and I needed him inside of me. It was like I was craving him. I'd always lowkey been a bit of a nympho, and Seth had clearly woken up the beast.

We fucked up until the time came for us to leave. We were flying out early because Seth had a big surgery Monday morning, and I had to be to work as well. It was a bittersweet feeling, but all good things had to come to an end.

We boarded the plane hand-in-hand like two high school sweethearts savoring the time we'd just spent together. The dick was good and all, but it was back to reality once this plane landed.

"So, if you're thinking 'bout ghosting a nigga, don't even try it," he said, looking away with a goofy grin on his face.

"...crazy 'cause I was thinking the same thing just now about you. You probably already got yo' phone on *Do Not Disturb,* ready to block all a bitch's calls," I laughed but was dead serious.

"Naw, my shit's all the way up, and you ain't gotta worry 'bout no calls being blocked 'cause I'ma be hitting yo' line too. So, *you* bet not start dodging me," he said, pressing the volume button on his phone to show me that it was forreal at its max.

We were up the whole plane ride talking about everything under sun—family, work, friendships, and past relationships. When the topic of why my most recent relationship ended came up, the tears began to effortlessly fall as I told him about Tristan's death.

"Ay, I'm sorry. If I would have known, I wouldn't have brought up such a sensitive subject," Seth apologized as I wiped my face and got myself together.

"No, I'm sorry for getting all emotional. I know that he's in a better place, and I'm finally learning how to move on," I told him, looking crazy from crying I'm sure.

When our flight finally landed back in San Francisco, we both groggily exited the plane with two separate cars waiting to take us home. I had texted Janae once it was okay to and let her know our time of arrival.

The stars were shining bright in the dark sky as we made our way onto the pavement and stood face-to-face with each other. Looking over, I smiled once I saw the girls waiting for me before turning my attention back to Seth. His hands were shoved into his pockets as the cold San Francisco air brushed past us. Bringing me close into

161

his body, he brought his arms around me before placing a kiss on my lips.

"Text me and let me know you made it home safe. I'll be waiting up 'til I hear from you," he said in a low deep tone as he pulled away from me.

After saying our final goodbyes, I entered the back of my car to find Mikel grilling the fuck out of me.

"Bitches think they grown and can just disappear for days at a time, huh? You need yo' ass whooped, hoe. You lucky you glowing, or I would've fa sho popped yo' ass. Now, down to business, bitch. Spill the tea…did you do a split on the dick or nah?" he asked as we all started cracking up. Everyone was all ears as Janae maneuvered the car out of the parking lot.

"Fuck a spilt, y'all, he picked me up! I'm talking 'bout no shaking or wavering, nothing. This man confidently picked me up before feasting on pussy. See, let me stop for I give y'all a full-on play by play. Just know a bitch got her game *all* the way woke up."

"Hoe, you really tried it. We need to hear about the nigga's dick and if he know how to work it. Bitch, you better get to spillin' the *real* tea," Mikel said unsatisfied with my response.

"I don't suck and tell," I said, playfully trying to hold back my laughter, "Nah, okay, honestly, y'all, the nigga is so big that I was truly a bit scared at first. It's been a little minute or whatever, and I thought he was gon' rip my ass open, but he was gentle and took his time. He made sure that he wasn't hurting me and fucked me in positions I didn't even know about. He was just really a true gentleman," I told them as everyone eagerly listened.

"Don't go catching feelings and getting in too deep too soon, Fe. I know how you can get. Just let him show you how he feels about you. Don't be the first to reveal your hand," Mikel told me knowing that I'm always quick to wear my heart on my sleeve.

"Well, Fe, I'm just glad to hear that you had fun. I know that you've been needing to let your hair down. And don't be scared to reveal your feelings; that often forces the other person to reveal theirs too. Just do whatever makes you happy at the end of the day because you, more than anyone I know, deserve that," Shanice spoke as she turned around to look at me, causing a smile to form on my face.

The girls dropped me off first before taking Mikel home, so we all said our goodbyes before I called it a night.

*****

Waking up the next morning, I felt like a new woman. I got up before my alarm even went off and Wiz Khalifa's "B.A.R." was blaring throughout the house as I got ready. Having just finished brushing my teeth, I was smoking a blunt before I showered as a text message came through on my phone. It was from a number I didn't recognize and contained a picture. Hitting the weed, I skeptically opened the message before dropping my phone.

The picture was of Tristan with his eyes wide open, leaking from the multiple gunshot wounds he sustained. Anger and sadness coursed through my veins as silent tears fell from my eyes, and my knees buckled beneath me. There was only one person who could've sent this to me, and he was obviously trying to send a message. I definitely heard him loud and clear, but, now, it was time for me to send mine. I thought waiting for someone else

163

to take care of this for me was the best option, but today let me know that this was personal. I had to finally put this nigga in his place, and only I could do it the way Tristan would have wanted me to.

Picking my phone back up, I wiped my tears and stood up on my feet. Today was a great day to put a bitch in their grave, and nothing else mattered at this point.

Pulling out a bag of weed, I rolled another blunt before calling Shanice and Janae, inviting them over to reveal the plan I had. Sitting down in front of my desktop, I connected my phone to try and unlock the IP address that was associated with the text message I received. I knew Josiah wouldn't be dumb enough to send that from his own phone, so I figured it was either a burner or one of those internet text messaging apps. As I worked my magic and traced the message to an online account, I found just what I needed as the doorbell rang. I knew it was the girls, so I hurried to answer and let them inside. With an excited grin on my face, I led the way, so they could follow me back to my room where I was smoking blunt after blunt.

"Fe, what's going on? You good?" Janae asked as she looked around my room and the thick smoke cloud that filled it.

"Yes, I'm good. I called you guys here because I need your help with something," I told them as they both took a seat on my bed.

Moving my attention from the computer and back to them, I took a deep breath in as I told them what I was planning to do and where they fit in.

"Fe, you know we got your back, but you sure about doing this alone? You don't wanna call Mikel or any of Tristan's men? How you know he ain't gon' have hella niggas at his spot?" Janae asked, being the first to speak up.

Not saying any words, I just walked into my closet and came back holding two fifty-cal desert eagles, one in each of my hands, as I pointed them in their direction. Walking back inside, I came back out holding a big body AK-47 in one hand and an AR-15 in the other. With one of our shipments, Emiliano included a case of guns as a gift, and I had been waiting to use them.

"I can keep going if y'all want. No matter how many niggas he got up in that bitch, I got something for them all. I just need to know that if shit gets real, y'all won't be too far behind and that y'all vow to lay down anything moving. I'm doing this shit with or without y'all, but I'd love to have y'all with me," I told them as I placed the guns back in my closet before taking a seat back at my computer desk.

"Oh, bitch, I'm down, but you gotta let me get one of them big bitches you got in there. I've wanted to shoot one of those for the longest," Shanice said excitedly as she jumped up from the bed and looked in my closet.

"I'm with you too, Fe, but if anything happens to you, I'm telling your crazy-ass best friend that I ain't heard from you in days, and if 12 comes knocking at my door, I don't know shit," Janae spoke as she joined Shanice in checking out the new guns.

Focusing my attention back on the computer screen, I found the IP address before quickly pulling up my command center to trace it to an actual location. The house was located in Antioch and wasn't too far of a drive from here. I just needed the day to fade, and like a thief in the night, I was coming for his ass.

Getting up, I picked up my phone and decided to call my baby brother. It had been a few days since I talked to

165

him, and I wanted to see how things were going using the drones.

"Wassup, sis?" he answered after the line rang twice.

"Shit, you know how my boring-ass do…got my head always buried in some work. I was just calling because I wanted to see how shit's been using the drones. Y'all tested them out yet?" I asked as I sealed another blunt closed and instantly sparked it.

"Sounds like you smoking…I was just finna roll up too," he chuckled before continuing. "But, everything's been going smooth, sis. All we been doing is really sitting back and watching the money come through at this point. This shit right here is the future of the game. Ain't nobody moving how we moving. We just gotta stay off the radar of the Feds, and this shit finna take our *shmoney* to the next level," he spoke, sounding like he was inhaling smoke.

"That's good-ass news, brah. I needed to hear this today…so once you make your move back to the Bay, we finna take this shit over. Like Beans from *State Property* said, 'These niggas can either get down or lay down,'" I told him as I walked over to my closet and passed the blunt to Janae. Her and Shanice were still sitting inside taking the guns apart and putting them back together. Them bitches were having way too much fun.

"It's all good, sis. We've been manufacturing more drones, and we're constantly monitoring everything. Once we touch down in the Bay, shit's gon' be sweet."

"A'ight…and I've been touching up a few things with the app on my end, making sure shit is straight, so we'll be good. Stay safe, and I love you, lil' bro," I told him as I walked to the kitchen to grab a bottle of water.

"Love you mo', sis," he replied before ending the call.

Standing in my kitchen drinking my water, I was in deep thought. I never wanted someone dead before or wished death on anyone, but this nigga Josiah had turned me into a new woman. Taking away the love of my life was like him ripping my heart right out of my chest. It was unforgivable and damn sho wouldn't go unnoticed. He'd been walking this earth for way too long while my baby was six-feet under.

Looking at the clock, time was moving so slowly. I had to do something to make occupy my mind.

Walking back into the room, I slid into some black jeans and a plain white tee. I was tired of sitting around, so I decided to go scope out the scene before everything went down tonight. Making my way into closet, I grabbed my white and black Jordan 9s as both Shanice and Janae looked at me skeptically.

"Where you going, Fe?" Shanice asked, looking up at me as they sat on the floor still messing with the guns.

"I just need to grab a few things from the store. I'll be right back. Y'all can chill here...y'all know where the weed and everything is," I said before grabbing one of the desert eagles and tucking it behind my back as I'd seen Tristan do so many times before.

"You need *that* to go to the store?" Janae quizzed.

"Yes, bitch, you never know...ain't nobody finna catch me slipping."

"Well, if you think it's ugly like that, maybe, we should come with you," she added, standing to her feet.

"I'm good, y'all. I'm just tryna be safe rather than sorry. I'll be right back," I told them with finality as I grabbed my keys and made my way towards the door.

Hopping into my all-black Range Rover, I wasted no time before backing out of my driveway and inputting the address into my GPS.

167

As I rode down the street, thoughts of Seth crossed my mind. He hadn't hit me up today and didn't respond when I texted him last night. The nigga was probably just tryna get some pussy anyway, but that was cool with me. I honestly just needed the dick, and, now that my head was clear, I was ready to come at these niggas full-speed.

Looking at the clock on my dash, I saw that it had just made 3 o'clock as I made my way to the freeway. Finally turning on the radio, Mozzy's blasted throughout the car.

"It's a beautiful struggle. I had to watch my mama suffer. They just popped my little brother. It's a beautiful struggle. My little sister on duffle 'cause her baby daddy a hustler. It's a beautiful struggle. I promise to come from nothin', but they made sure I ain't walk for nothin'. It's a beautiful struggle. I said beautiful 'cause I love it. After this, we ain't doin' no more strugglin', move you out of the struggle."

I rapped along to every word as I pushed through traffic knowing in my heart that, after this, there wouldn't be no more struggling. Emotionally, I would be at peace.

The music faded as my GPS came through instructing me to exit off on Lone Tree Way. Exiting off the freeway into a nice suburban area, I made a left turn up a street called Deer Trails Drive where there was nothing but massive houses all down the block. They all had to have at least five-bedrooms, and I was honestly shocked that Josiah was living like this. Had him killing Tristan really elevated his money like this? Anger coursed through my body as I realized this nigga was eating as a result of killing my fiancé.

Slowing rolling down the street, my GPS told me that the destination was on the right before I came to a stop.

He had the biggest house on the block, and it was surrounded by a huge black gate. His house looked like two houses combined, and there were security cameras everywhere. Sitting in my car across the street, I watched as the gates opened and out came Nalia and Talia. They both were walking to a teal-colored Audi but were stopped when Josiah walked out. He approached Talia, placing a firm smack on her ass before placing a kiss on her lips. Then, he walked over to Nalia's side and did the same thing to her, causing my mouth to drop.

So, this nigga is fucking them both? I thought. Had Nalia been playing me or what? My mind was racing as I thought about what type of plan they could've had for my ass.

Leaning my seat all the way back, I ducked as I noticed them pulling out of the driveway. Waiting until they got a decent distance ahead, I started my car back up and followed behind them. Nalia was supposed to killing that nigga, but, from the looks of things, his ass had been killing her pussy.

Making sure that I stayed at least three-cars behind, I tailed them until they reached Nalia's apartment. Waiting until they were out of the cars and inside the entrance, I grabbed my desert eagle and a silencer from out of my glovebox before I stepped out of the car. Tucking the gun behind my back, I made sure to blend in as I entered the building and made my way towards the elevators. Getting on with an elderly couple, I pressed the fifth-floor before the doors closed behind us, and we were on our way up.

When the doors opened on the fifth-floor, I walked out into the hallway and could hear their voices. They must have just entered the apartment. Listening in, I heard Nalia say, "That bitch Felicia really thought my ass was finna pick her side over my blood's."

That was all I needed to hear as I slowly turned the knob and found that the door was unlocked. Quietly, I pushed it open in stealth mode as I saw the guest bathroom door close and water running behind it.

"Damn, bitch...took yo' ass long enough to find me a face towel," Talia said undressing as she had her back turned to me.

With no remorse, I lifted my gun, aiming it at her head before splattering her brains all over the beautiful brown and turquoise shower curtain. Her body instantly dropped to the ground like literal dead weight as I turned and made my way to the back of the house. I felt no emotion as continued to move stealthy before hearing Nalia come my way.

Getting behind a wall, I waited until she got into clear view before I moved quickly, smashing the butt of the gun into her face as she stumbled back confused.

"Fe?" she questioned with blood now leaking from her nose into her mouth rapidly. I didn't respond as I brought the gun back in front of me, pointing it at the center of her chest. "Fe, wassup, bitch? I was 'bout to take care of that for you tonight. What type of shit you on?" she asked, looking genuinely muddled as a smile crept onto my face.

"Oh, I see...so you thought playing both sides of the fence wouldn't come back to bite yo' ass? You of all people should know the last thing I am is stupid. I saw you kissing on Josiah, letting the nigga smack yo' ass like he just ran up in you. What? Y'all was finna be some weird-ass, dysfunctional, throuple?" I laughed. "Well, don't let me stop y'all. All you bitches can now burn together in hell. Your sister is already waiting on you, and your nigga will be joining you soon. Sweet dreams, bitch," I gritted before pulling the trigger, knocking her back into the wall as blood started spilling from both her chest and mouth.

Walking over to her body, I pumped one more into her to make sure she was no longer breathing. Searching the house, I hurried to find their car keys before tucking my gun and making my way out of the apartment as quick as I came. Luckily, when I stepped back out into the hallway, no one was present. Moving quickly, I pressed the elevator button repeatedly before the doors finally opened. Once I made it back down to the lobby, I took the back exit and briskly walked around the block to the parking garage. Grabbing my phone from the Range Rover, I locked my doors before climbing into Talia's 2019 Audi A7. I knew I was tripping getting into a dead bitch's car, but this was a sure way for me to get into the gate Josiah had around his home.

Picking up the phone, I called Janae and let her know what was up before texting them the address. I also instructed her ass to grab a duffle bag and fill it with all the guns we had in the closet and to bring me an all-black sweat suit.

Making my way back to Antioch from Oakland where Nalia and Talia's apartment was, I road in silence the whole way. The anticipation of bodying this nigga Josiah was at an all-time high, and I couldn't wait.

Looking at my lock screen, I saw a picture of Tristan grinning as he stood in front of his old jets.

"All of this is for you, baby. After tonight, you can finally rest in peace," I spoke aloud as silent tears fell from my eyes. Shaking them off quickly, I focused my attention back on the road as the picture of him sitting lifelessly in the car flashed through my mind.

Gripping the steering wheel, I floored my foot on the gas as I become enraged. Josiah had killed a real man, so his bitch-ass could be living lavish off my nigga's name.

Exiting off the freeway, I turned up on Deer Trails once more before parking on the side street, cutting the lights off, and sitting back. It was now 7:30 p.m., and the sun had already set. Sitting in the car under the pitch-black sky, I waited until I saw headlights pull up behind me and knew it was the girls. Hopping out of Talia's car, I saw the look of concern on both their faces, but they said nothing as Janae handed me the clothes to change into. Pulling my jeans off, I hurried to put the sweat suit on as I told them once more what the plan was.

"There's a gate opener in her car, so I'll be able to get in with no problem. Once I'm in, I want y'all to wait 'til the gate is 'bout to close, then pull in behind me. I need y'all to be ready when y'all feet touch this pavement again. We don't know what these niggas finna be on. If you see a mothafucka even blink, I want you to drop they ass on sight. We good?" I asked, moving to the trunk of their car where I knew the duffle bag was. Grabbing the AK, I said nothing else to them as I climbed back behind the wheel and started Talia's car up. Turning on the lights, I turned the music on, and Money Bagg Yo came through the speakers.

"I gotta thang for bitches. I don't really hang with bitches, but if you see me with 'em, nine times outta ten, I'm banging them bitches."

Reaching above me, I pressed the gate opener as the huge steel gates opened, allowing me entrance. Pulling into the steep driveway, I was surprised to see that I was greeted by no one. Parking in the garage, I made enough space for the girls to get in. Grabbing the AK, I exited the car fearlessly before wasting no time entering the home through the garage door. As I made my way inside, I found some niggas big chilling, playing an intense game of 2K19. They were kicked back like they didn't have a soul who could touch them, but boy were these niggas wrong. Hell had no fury like a woman scorned.

Holding the automatic gun up, I pulled the trigger, sending a spray of bullets all across the living room slumping them both. They were just so joyously engaged in the game and now lay there lifelessly as blood seeped from their wounds.

"Bitch, niggas," I spat before coming around the corner to a huge spiral staircase. I was just about to make my way up them when I felt a presence behind me. Instantly, I turned around on full alert to find Seth holding a twelve-gauge shot gun aimed at my head. Stunned, I looked at him in pure astonishment as he shrugged his shoulders in return.

"It ain't personal, Fe…it's just business," I heard him say before I heard a loud gunshot and saw a bright flash before everything went dark.

To be continued…

Calling all authors...
We want to read your book!

Black Eden Publications is currently looking for the best of the best to join our squad. Do you think you have what it takes to become an Insider? If you are a dope writer, we would love to hear from you. Let us see what you got!

www.blackedenpublications.com/submissions

#shopblack

BLACK EDEN PUBLICATIONS

Please send order form to:
P.O. Box 128, Mount Eden, CA 94557
info@blackedenpublications.com

Thank you for your order!

Shipping Information:

Date: ___ / ___ / ___

Name: _____

Address: _____

Email: _____

City/State/Zip: _____ _____ _____

Pricing:

    a.   Shipping + $3.00

    b.   Receive a 15% discount when you order **5 or more books** during the same order.

Title	Price	#	Total
A Murderous Affair	$15.00		$
Betrayal in the City	$15.00		$
Boy Toy	$15.00		$
City Nights	$15.00		$
Cocoa Baby	$15.00		$
Counterfeit Dreams	$15.00		$
Counterfeit Dreams 2: A Hustler's Hope	$15.00		$
Counterfeit Dreams 3: A Dream's Nightmare	$15.00		$
Counterfeit Dreams 4: A Coke White Dream	$15.00		$
Counterfeit Dreams 5: When Dreams Aren't Enough	$15.00		$
Counterfeit Dreams 6: Dreams Never Die	$15.00		$
Counterfeit Dreams: The Complete Collection	$75.00		$
Dying for Change	$15.00		$
He's Got a Hold on Me	$12.50		$
He's Got a Hold on Me 2	$15.00		$

"Welcome to the Inner Circle..."

Let's Be Friends	$15.00		$
One Man's Trash	$15.00		$
Rose Petals Under a Reaper's Robe	$12.50		$
Rose Petals Under a Reaper's Robe Unveiled	$12.50		$
Shade Built My Empire	$15.00		$
Ski Mask Divas	$15.00		$
Ski Mask Schemes: The Prequel	$15.00		$
The Diary of She	$12.50		$
The Diary of She – Vol. II: Poems & Affirmations	$12.50		$
The Future of the Dope Game	$15.00		$
Trap Goddess	$15.00		$
Twisted: The Short Story	$10.00		$
What Bae Don't Know	$15.00		$
	Total		$

Payment (Check appropriate box):

☐ Money Order

☐ Check

☐ Pay Using Credit Card (Please contact info@blackedenpublications.com for invoice)